RESPECT REVENGE Pt. 1

"WHEN NAPTOWN COULDN'T SLEEP"

H.a.r.d. P.a.r.t.

Publishing

RESPECT REVENGE Pt. 1
"When Naptown Couldn't Sleep"

Copyright © 2009 by H.A.R.D. P.A.R.T. Publishing

All Rights Reserved

This book is a work of fiction. Names, characters, businesses, organizations, places, events, and incidents either are the product of the author's imagination or are used fictitiously. Any resemblance to actual persons, living or dead, events, or locales is entirely coincidental.

ISBN 978-0-69-276424-4

Printed in the United States of America

RESPECT REVENGE Pt. 1
"When Naptown Couldn't Sleep"

DEDICATION

To My sister who is no longer with me in flesh, but will always be with me in mind and spirit…
Lakeisha R. Williams

1981-2000

RESPECT REVENGE Pt. 1
"When Naptown Couldn't Sleep"

ACKNOWLEDGMENTS

First and Foremost, I give all thanks to the God who dwells within me. Without a strong sense of spirituality, an understanding of truth and a definitive belief in SELF, none of this would be possible. I must give honor and recognition to the woman who raised me and showed me the meaning of the term unconditional love; none other than my grandmother Carlene F. Stevens. To my beautiful, loving, caring, supportive and very dedicated wife, your belief in me inspires me to be the best me I can be on a daily basis. Last but not least, I have to pay homage and respect to the streets I grew up running. These are your stories I'm telling. I love Naptown from one side to the other, but I rep the West-Side and more specifically The Hard-Part!!! I do it for the streets and we in here!!! 100

RESPECT REVENGE Pt. 1
"When Naptown Couldn't Sleep"

SHOCK-G

RESPECT REVENGE Pt. 1
"When Naptown Couldn't Sleep"

CHAPTER 1

"Mutha fucka!" I'm in a fucked up position right now. I'm way too street smart and been through way too much to have let this shit go down like this. Now that I think about it, I saw all the signs, but we be moving so fast in them streets that some shit slips right by us. I'm not the first to be in this position, nor will I be the last, but I figured if I tell you how I got here, then I might be able to help you avoid it. I gotta start at the beginning so it will all make sense in the end. It was the summer of 89' and I was eleven years old and I lived on the eastside of Indianapolis with my grandmother, Caroline. She was hands down the sweetest, most kind-hearted person in the world in my eyes. I mean, this woman would give you the shirt off her back if you were without. She had legal guardianship of me from the time I was six months old, so she basically raised me from the dirt. My father lived in the same house, but he was a big grown ass kid himself; That's probably why he was 29 years old still living in his mother's basement. My pop's was only 18 when he got my mother pregnant on a one night stand they had after a neighborhood house party. She was only 16 and the daughter

RESPECT REVENGE Pt. 1
"When Naptown Couldn't Sleep"

of a strict local preacher who didn't want to be the laughing stock of his whole congregation, let him tell it. So him and his wife decided to hide it from everyone until the baby was born, then they would decide what to do about it. Once I was born, they forced my mom to make a tough decision and gave her only six months to do it, ... Give her child up for adoption, or get out and get her own place. At 16 years old in 1978, that was not an easy thing to do, so she did what she thought was best, ... She put me on my grandmother porch and simply walked away. To granny I wasn't a burden, but a blessing and she been there for a nigga ever since.

By then my family only consisted of five people and we all stayed under one roof. There was me, my pops, my granny, Auntie Rhonda and her daughter Keisha. My granny had a room, I had a room, Auntie and Keisha shared one, and my old man stayed in the basement. I remember how it all started ... I was down in the basement watching my father shave his face. Looking at him was like seeing an older version of myself, I looked exactly like the cat. My old man stood 6'3 and was about 200 pounds solid, brown skinned with broad shoulders, and a bald head. I was sitting there in my feelings because he was getting ready to go over his girlfriend's house, again. He had been over there every day, all day, for the last few weeks. He usually stayed around the house and fucked wit me all the time, but lately this chic had him more than I did. He asked me,
"Why are you sitting over there looking so sad?"
"Because I thought we was going to play the video game together and now you leaving again!"
"Well, you won't have to worry about me leaving to see her pretty soon because we will be getting married in two months and we are all getting our own place." All I could think to say was, "What about granny? "

RESPECT REVENGE Pt. 1
"When Naptown Couldn't Sleep"

"There is a time in every mans' life when he needs to leave the nest and be a man, you know, start his own family. Now that I've met a good God-fearing woman, it's my time." Then he added, "So you with me or not?"
"Yeah, I guess I'm with it."
"Well, gone upstairs and I'll see you when I get back."
I turned and ran up the steps two at a time. When I got to the top of the steps, I could hear the theme music to the video game Super Mario Brothers coming from my room. That meant my lil cousin Keisha was in my room again. I didn't like her in my room when I wasn't with her, she didn't know how to handle the video games right. Keisha was a cute lil light-skinned girl with hazel eyes and fat cheeks. She wore her hair in a lot of lil ponytails with colorful balls all over the place. To everybody else in the house, she could do no wrong, but I knew better, the little girl was bad as hell when wasn't nobody looking. So every chance I got, I made her pay. I snuck up behind her and pulled one her ponytails real hard.
"OUCH!" "Eric, I'm telling grandma on you!"
"I don't care; you shouldn't be in my room anyway!"
"This ain't yo room no more cause my granny said you and your daddy getting y'all own house and this gonna be my room, so now ugly!"
"Who you callin' ugly? Yo momma ugly!"
That's all she needed to hear.
"Aw, I'm telling, you called my momma ugly! Momma, Eric called you ugly!" I ran out behind her yelling,
"No I didn't Auntie Rhonda, she lying, she always trying to get me in trouble!"
Auntie was sitting on her bed painting her toe nails when we burst in.
    She said, "I know one thang, y'all bout to get on my

RESPECT REVENGE Pt. 1
"When Naptown Couldn't Sleep"

nerves!" "Both of y'all get y'all little ugly selves somewhere and sit down!"
Auntie had to be the most beautiful woman in the whole world. She was tall for a woman at five foot nine, and had pretty gold skin with silky hair that fell down to her shoulders. She didn't wear no make-up at all, just lip gloss and she was still the best looking woman around. Some black folk like to lie and say they had Indian in their blood, but Auntie looked like the opposite. She looked like an Indian with some Black in her blood. We were messing up her pre-club ritual of painting her toe nails, while listening to Whitney Houston, so she put us in our places real quick.
"Keisha you go in there with momma and you take yo lil nappy headed self in there and run you some bath water!"
When we got back in the hallway, I pulled her hair again and ran off to do as I was told. After that, the rest of the summer was pretty uneventful, ... a lot of playing with Keisha, riding my bike up and down the street and playing Nintendo. Then in September, my pops had a small wedding at the church we all went to and then me, him, and his new wife Sharon moved to the Westside on a street called Harding. Little did I know; life would never be the same ...

RESPECT REVENGE Pt. 1
"When Naptown Couldn't Sleep"

CHAPTER
2

Indianapolis or "Nap-Town" as it is called in the underworld, is not what you see on TV. If you listen to the media, you would believe that we were all about the Colts and the Pacers or the Indianapolis 500. We also host one of the biggest Black Expos in the country. Stars fly in from all around to attend and mingle with masses. I'll admit, all of the above is true, but what they don't tell you is that our geographical location makes us a major thoroughfare for drugs taking cross country trips. Everybody knows where there are drugs, there is money, and where there is money, there are guns, and where there are guns, there's murder. Nap-town is the eleventh largest city in the country. The city is broken down into 5 sections. You got the East and West side, the North and South side, then you got downtown. The Northside and downtown are dominated by white people and upper class black folk. The Southside is populated by the low class whites that are only different from the ghetto blacks by the skin color and location. The East and West sides are all black…and I mean all black. But the Westside is definitely the grimiest, most dangerous side of all. There is a street called Harding on the Westside of "Nap-

RESPECT REVENGE Pt. 1
"When Naptown Couldn't Sleep"

Town" and it's the main strip in da hood known as "The Hard Part." Living on Harding was a whole new experience for me, I mean, everywhere you looked, there were broke down cars with all the windows busted, every other house on every block was abandoned, or should have been. Spray paint was on every inch of every wall in sight and every corner was packed with people hangin' out drinkin' smokin' and whatever else they wanted. Harding seemed like it was the exact opposite of where we had moved from on the eastside. This shit was gutter, fo' real!

Our first night in our new place was my first time hearing live gunshots. My dumb ass ran to the window expecting to see the night sky light up because I assumed the series of pops to be fireworks. My step mother was terrified, she told my father,
"Big Ed, I don't like it here and I do not feel safe!"
He said, "Baby, be cool, I'm sure it's not this live around here every night, plus Daddy gonna protect his family."
He looked at me with a wink and a smile.
"Let's give it a chance and if it's that bad then we will look for something else."
That seemed to satisfy her a little bit.
I kind of liked our street because there were plenty of young boys always running up and down the block. I sat on the porch for the first few days and just watched because I couldn't go nowhere yet, my pops wanted to learn the hood before he turned me loose.

On the way to the bus stop on my first day of school, I read the sprayed on gang signs on every wall. There were only two phrases that kept popping up, "The Bottom Boyz" and "The Hard Part." While I was reading the wall of the building on the corner where I was supposed to catch the bus, this lil dude walked up on me talkin' bout,
"What's up my man, where you from?"
This lil nigga looked like he hadn't had a bath in days. He was

RESPECT REVENGE Pt. 1
"When Naptown Couldn't Sleep"

a lil nappy head, dirty, charcoal black mufucka wit big teeth. He was about the same age as I was, but he was kind of on the small side. I answered,
"I just moved down on Harding."
"So you new around here, huh?"
"Yeah, I guess so."
"Well, I'm Lil Smurf and I run it round here."
 When he said that, the three lil flunkies he had with him burst out laughing at his comment. I told him my name was Eric, then tried to walk on past him, he blocked my path by stepping in front of me and his partners started to try and surround me. My pops had told me that I would probably have to fight a couple of times, just to show that I would, and my gut told me this was one of 'em. I swung as hard as I could at the closest one to me and then took off running. My punch caught Lil Smurf somewhere in the face causing him to stumble back a lil bit. I made it about half a block before I felt a hand pull me to the ground by the back of my shirt,
"You can't get away you bitch ass nigga!"
Lil Smurf was trying to put me in the head lock, but I slipped out of it somehow and ended up on top of him. It must have been fear that gave me strength because I was all over this dude. I was giving him the business, and felt like he couldn't do nothing wit me until one of his lil buddies ran up behind me and grabbed me around the neck, putting me in the sleeper hold. I tried to grab his arm to get him up off of me, but it was too late, he had it locked in. Lil Smurf jumped up and started giving me his best shots, all to the head and face. Then all of a sudden shit just went black.
        When I came too, the young boys were gone and so was the few dollars I had gotten from my old man to eat lunch, but there was this big black dude standing over me trying to help me

RESPECT REVENGE Pt. 1
"When Naptown Couldn't Sleep"

get it together. "Lil man, get up, you a'ight?"
When he finally got me focused and helped me to my feet, I could feel that my forehead had a knot on it, and my lip was busted and bleeding. The big guy told me,
    "Come on, follow me, I got some ice in the crib."
 I said, "I ain't going in yo house for no ice, I don't even know you."
"Lil nigga I ain't gonna do you no harm, I saw the whole situation go down from my porch and I came and ran the lil gangstas off when shit got out of hand."
"You waited kind of long didn't you?" I asked out of frustration.
"I had to see how you would handle the situation before I stepped in. I like how you dealt wit that, but you should have been a little faster." He laughed at his lil joke then said,
"Now come on in here and wash yo face off."
 I followed the O.G. into his crib and he pointed me to the bathroom and told me,
 "Get a towel out the closet and then come on in the kitchen, I got ice in here."
When I got to the kitchen the big fella was standing there smoking a joint,
 "You smoke, lil man?"
"Naw, I'm only eleven."
"You would be surprised at how young they start these days, but anyway, I'm Big June, so you new around here, huh?"
"Yea, how you know?"
"It's my job to know everybody and anybody around here and I ain't never seen you."
"Yeah, I just moved around the corner wit my daddy."
"Well, welcome to the Hard Part, baby! You better get ready to fight them lil niggas every time you see 'em or stay in the house!"
"I ain't staying in no house!" He let out a lil laugh, then said,

RESPECT REVENGE Pt. 1
"When Naptown Couldn't Sleep"

"I like that, you a lil nigga wit some heart, so this is what I'm gonna do. I'm a take you to your crib right now, but in the morning when you come to your bus stop, I'll be waiting on you, then we will take care of this."

Later that day, I was at home waiting on my daddy to get there from work. Sharon was talking big shit about how much trouble I was in and how I was going to get it for being around here fighting and for not going to school.
"You need to go to your room until Big Ed get here."
So I slid off to my room until I heard my old man come through the door.
"What's up, family?"
"I'll tell you what's up, Eric been round here fighting, and he missed school because of it."
"Well, did he win or what?"
"This ain't funny, Big Ed, he ain't got no business fightin.'" Then he turned to me,
"What happened, baby boy?" I put on my pitiful face and told my story,
"These lil dudes walked up on me while I was waiting on my bus and tried to jump me. I punched one of 'em and then took off running. They chased me and jumped me, but I got one of 'em good."
I purposely left out everything about Big June, I didn't feel like hearing the "never talk to strangers" speech again. He asked me was I alright, then took a look at the knot on my head and told me,
"You did right by fighting back, if you didn't fight, then you would be getting chased home every day."
Sharon was hot as fish grease cause she was expecting him to be mad or punish me, but the truth was, he had never raised his voice at me, and damn sure wasn't doin' no whoopins'.

RESPECT REVENGE Pt. 1
"When Naptown Couldn't Sleep"

The next morning, I left for the bus stop not knowing what to expect. From a distance I could see a bunch of kids, but couldn't make out no faces. Then I heard somebody call my name,
"Lil Eric, come here."
I turned around and Big June was walking towards me with the dirtiest mufucka I had ever seen. My first thought was, this dude got to be a bum. All of his teeth were brown or missing, his lips were dry as hell and white like he had baby powder on 'em. It looked like if he smiled too hard they would crack and start bleeding. His eyes were yellow and his clothes looked like he had been wearing them for about a month. Then to my surprise, the bum handed Big June a fifty-dollar bill, then said,
"Come on June, hook my shit up, that's my last, plus I been spending all night." Big June handed him something I couldn't quite see and my man turned and damn near took off running down the alley. Then Big June turned his attention back to me,
"Come on Lil E, let's go see what these lil niggas talkin' bout."
I said, "Big June who was that bum you was talking too?"
"That so called bum is how I eat and you too young to be trying to question an O.G. anyway."
I didn't know what he meant by that's how he ate, so I just left it at that because dude didn't look like the type of stud whose bad side you wanted to be on. He was a big ole dude, 6 foot 5 and 300 pounds. Yeah, he was a little on the hefty side, but definitely wasn't sloppy wit it; he was a solid mufucka. He wore his hair in neat cornrows to the back and you could tell he was gangsta just by his demeanor. As we approached the crowd of youngsters, he yelled out,
"Hey, Lil Smurf, my man right here trying to see you one on one."

RESPECT REVENGE Pt. 1
"When Naptown Couldn't Sleep"

As soon as he said it, my stomach dropped. I thought maybe he planned on making sure I got on the bus safe or would talk it out with the dude or something. Smurf answered,

"Yeah, I'll see him one on one, I whooped him yesterday, I'm a whoop him today, and I might just whoop him tomorrow!" His whole clique laughed at that one. I'll give him one thing for sure, ... he had a slick mouth on him. That's when I noticed there were kids from other bus stops out there, they had come to see a show. Everybody had been waiting on me. Lil Smurf took off his jacket and shirt and squared up on me. I handed my book bag to Big June and walked up on Lil Smurf, I was nervous and anxious and didn't see no sense in stallin'. My man wasted no time settin' it off! He swung a wild right hand at my face and caught me on the side of the head. I'm left handed, so he never saw my wild one coming! I connected with his jaw and made him stagger back a few steps. Right then I saw something in his eyes that told me he had realized that this wasn't going to be easy and that gave me more confidence. He rushed me and we ending up rolling around on the ground. I heard kids yelling,

"Get him Lil Smurf, kick his ass!"

Some were even rootin' for me. I guess since he had been the lil bully of the hood for youngins, seein' somebody finally give him his medicine gave them a lil hope. Somehow we ended up back on our feet and were trading punches and then it happened. He swung real wild and missed and damn near fell in the middle of the street. I didn't give him time to recover, I got on his ass and let the blows go from all angles. It seemed like I was unconscious, just swinging for the fences. When I was too tired to swing another punch, I realized that he was on the ground covering his head with both arms trying to protect his face. Everybody out there was quiet; they couldn't believe the new dude had just whooped Lil Smurf. Big June went over and helped him up and made sure

RESPECT REVENGE Pt. 1
"When Naptown Couldn't Sleep"

he was alright, then said,
    "Now y'all shake hands, y'all from the same hood now, my hood, so y'all might as well get used to it."
It shocked me when the lil bastard extended his hand towards me. I reached out for it and he pulled it back and hit me dead in the mouth. I saw nothing but stars and heard him say,
    "Now, we even, nigga."
I regained my composure and then extended my hand and said,
    "Since we even now, let's squash it then."
He must have thought I was going to play him how he played me because he was skeptical about the hand shake, but he slowly stuck his hand out and we shook up. I didn't know it right then, but this dude was going to be one of my closest comrades.
    I had been around here for a couple of weeks, been jumped once, and won an important fight. I didn't have them kind of problems no more, I was now accepted in The Hard Part ...

RESPECT REVENGE Pt. 1
"When Naptown Couldn't Sleep"

CHAPTER 3

Life on Harding was not as bad as we thought it would be. My old man was working at Pepsi Cola and Sharon was working at a bank, so they were making decent money and we weren't struggling as bad as a lot of the people around us. My pops even went out and got a slightly used "88 Thunderbird." Being that it was only a couple of years old, that was like a Benz in the hood. I was playing basketball every day, doing good in school, and whooping on Lil Smurf in video games. My father did a lot of shit with me back then and being that Lil Smurf was always around he even became a fixture in Lil Smurf's life. He went around to Lil Smurf's house and met his mother and seen that the conditions were not good around there, so he tried to make sure my guy had shoes and shit, plus he was invited to eat with us like every night. Lil Smurf's mother was a real bad alcoholic and she wasn't doing for herself or lil buddy, so he damn near lived with us.

  It was "91" by now and we had been out of granny's' house for two years, but I went over her house every other weekend. I loved my granny to death, plus I missed Auntie Rhonda and Keisha. I was over there this one weekend and

RESPECT REVENGE Pt. 1
"When Naptown Couldn't Sleep"

my old man never showed up to pick me up and I had to go to school the next day. So my granny called Sharon to tell her that I was on my way, then sent me home in a cab. When I walked in the door I could tell something was wrong because Sharon was sitting on the couch crying, her eyes were puffy and red and she wouldn't even look at me. I asked her, "What's wrong Sharon?" She didn't answer or even look up, so I changed my question, "Where my Daddy at?" She said she hadn't seen him since Friday night when he dropped me off at my granny's house. It turned out that he had been leaving the house every night that week after I went to bed, only to return just before it was time for me to get up and go to school. Now he had been gone for two days, something was definitely wrong.

Monday morning rolled around, still with no sign of pops. I got up and got ready for school and Sharon was getting ready for work like any other day but today we got ready in total silence. There were so many thoughts running through my mind, I just couldn't figure it out. I heard Sharon talking to somebody on the phone and heard her say,

"He probably got him a woman around here somewhere, and if he do, I will be leaving his ass!"

I was more worried that something had happened to him. I left for my bus stop and really didn't feel like going to school, when I saw Big June in his regular spot. I had been in the hood long enough now to know that the dudes I used to think were "Bums" were actually the neighborhood tweekers, crackheads, hypes or whatever else you could come with to call them, I now knew Big June hung on his front porch every morning and sold dope to the early morning geekers. Actually it was early morning to me, but they had been up and at it all night long, but what really fucked me up was when I saw my father pull up in the Thunderbird and flag Big June over to the car. June walked over

RESPECT REVENGE Pt. 1
"When Naptown Couldn't Sleep"

and got in for a few seconds and then got right back out, stickin money in his pocket. When I walked up on the car, my old man glanced over at me just long enough to make eye contact, looked away and pulled off squealing his tires. Big June looked at me and said,
>"What's up with him?"

>"That was my old man in that car."

>"Damn Lil E, I ain't know your pops was a smoker!"

>"I didn't either."

Then he said, "He been coming around here for about a week now."

I hung my head and headed on home. I didn't feel like going to school at first, but I really didn't feel like going now.

Later that night, my daddy came home looking a mess, and dead broke. He had just got paid that Friday. I heard him and Sharon arguing in their bedroom about where he had been, then he came out and slammed the door and went down in the basement. I waited about ten minutes and then went down after him. I got to the bottom of the steps and couldn't believe my eyes. He was sitting at a table in the corner with a big ass glass pipe up to his lips. I had never seen anybody smoke crack, but I had heard plenty of crack head stories living in the hood, and I knew that was what I was seeing right then. He looked up at me and dam near shitted on hisself. He got to fumbling around trying to hide this and that, but he was real careful with that pipe. He stuck it in a sock and gently slid it under the hot water heater. He walked over to me like he was tip toeing, trying to be quiet and said,

>"Where Sharon at? Do she know I'm down here? Did you tell her that you saw me earlier?"

Then he started lookin' around like it was more than just me and him down there. He was sweating real hard and still had on the same filthy clothes he had been wearing for three days. He bent

RESPECT REVENGE Pt. 1
"When Naptown Couldn't Sleep"

down and whispered to me,

"Man don't tell nobody what you saw okay? I'm just going through a thang right now, I'm a get myself together you hear me? You my boy, I know you can keep it between us. I been having you since you was six months old. Now go on over by that door and tell me if you hear her coming."

I couldn't believe this was happening. This was not my father sneaking around the basement smoking crack, and asking me, his thirteen-year-old son, to not only keep it between us, but be his look out so his wife didn't catch him. I was speechless and my heart was crushed. Silent tears rolled down my face as I headed to the steps to make sure my old man didn't get caught smoking his life away. He bent down to get his pipe from under the water heater, looked up at me to make sure all was clear, then sat back down at his table and changed both of our lives forever.

Needless to say, shit went downhill from there. Every time he got paid, he would be missing until Monday night. Then he would come home dead ass broke with the stupidest excuses I'd ever heard. It took Sharon maybe a whole month after that first episode to figure out it was more than just another woman. I guess coming home from work trying to cut on the lights and realizing they had been disconnected was a strong indicator. The gas was next, then he got the Thunderbird repossessed. That was the straw that broke the camel's back. Sharon packed her shit and told my man,

"You can destroy your life if you want to, but I'm not going to sit around and watch you do it!"

She promised to come back if he got his mind right. Needless to say, she never made it back. Once she left, he stopped trying to hide it from anybody. His appearance went to shit almost instantly, he had lost almost twenty or thirty pounds, said fuck a haircut or a shave, and wore the same jeans and sweatshirt every

RESPECT REVENGE Pt. 1
"When Naptown Couldn't Sleep"

fucking day. In just six months, my tall, handsome, vibrant, father had turned into every other zombie I saw walking around the hood.

Before long he started having his smoking buddies over to the house all the time and I would see them in groups of three or four, smoking at the table in the living room. So I would leave and hang wit Lil Smurf, sometimes we would roam the streets until three or four in the morning. We started to get into shit. We were riding our bikes up north and breaking into people houses, smoking weed, stealing cars, you name it, we were doing it. We even started selling candle wax and soap to the local fiends just to keep a lil change in our pockets. Big June caught wind of that and sent word for me to come and holla at him. He sat me down and explained how, if I had a little bit of dope, I could serve all of them smokers that be in and out of my crib. So he fronted me a lil fifty dollar break down and sent me around there. My old man tricked me out of my whole sack immediately. When I showed him what Big June had given me, he told me,

"Give it here and sit right here on the porch, I'm a make em' buy it and then bring you the money."

I fucked around and ended up sitting on that porch for hours before I realized I was beat.

By the time the summer of "92" rolled around, I was fourteen, years old and I had started hanging on the corner in front of Doc Tibbs variety store. This corner never slept. Besides the variety store, you also had a bar called the Ritz Lounge, a pool hall, and a numbers house. Where people play the ghetto lottery. Plus, this corner had any kind of drug you could think of. So much money passed through there every day and me and Smurf wasn't getting any of it. But I've always been a smart kid, so I watched the fiends, the hustlers, and the police. I wanted to know everything about everything. Then finally I saw my window

RESPECT REVENGE Pt. 1
"When Naptown Couldn't Sleep"

of opportunity and wasted no time jumping at my chance at a come up. This nigga named Taco use to come from another hood to shoot dice in the Hard-Part all the time. The hustlers from our hood stopped what they were doing to take shots at this nigga's bankroll. They would all give me five dollars apiece to watch out and holla "PO-PO" if the laws were coming. It would be about nine or ten players in the game, so I would make off with forty-five or fifty dollars easy. This particular day, the corner was in full swing, shit moving and shaking all around us. I copped me and Lil Smurf a dime bag of weed and was smoking a blunt while watching out for the police and watching the money in the dice game change hands at the same time. Lil Smurf was so broke he couldn't pay attention and it didn't bother him one bit, as long as we got us a sack of weed and had enough left over to get us a pizza or something, he was cool. I took a long drag of the blunt and came up with a plan.

"Lil Smurf we always stealing cars and riding around trying to break into something. I think it's time we move up in the food chain a lil bit."

"Man Lil E, you letting this weed go to your head!"

"It ain't the weed that's going to my head, it's the fact that we be out here all day and watch all this money be made and we ain't getting none unless we sell some fake dope or play look out while another nigga get money!"

Then Lil Smurf said, "So how do you propose we fix it since you so ready to move up in the world?"

I answered, "That nigga Taco. Don't nobody around here like that nigga and if we rob him ain't nobody gonna trip. We can come off with all that money he always flashing!"

Smurf answered, "We don't even got no gun or nothing."

"Yeah, but I know where we can get one real quick."

"Where you gonna get a gun from Lil E?"

RESPECT REVENGE Pt. 1
"When Naptown Couldn't Sleep"

I looked him in the eye and said, "From Lil Dave."
"Lil Dave ain't gonna give you his gun!"
"You think so huh? Well watch this."
Lil Dave was a regular in the dice game, plus he was Big June's right hand man. Big June front him dope and he push it off on everybody else. Anything that went on up on the corner, Lil Dave knew about it, then he would fill in Big June. That's why Lil Dave had been tellin' me to quit standing around watchin everything, "and get you some of this money!" He the one that told me it was time to move up in the food chain. So I stepped to him,
"Yo Lil Dave, let me holla at you for a minute!"
"What's good Lil E?"
I pulled him to the side and said, "You been tellin' me that I need to make a move and get some money in my pockets and now I'm ready, but I need your help."
"What you need fam?"
"I need your burner."
"What's going down that you need my burner?"
"I'm getting ready to rob that nigga Taco!"
He started laughing like I told a joke or something. I didn't know what was so funny so I asked him,
"What's so funny?"
He said, "So you serious huh?" You really want that kinda drama? You know that nigga might want to get at you about that and you gotta be ready and willing to deal wit that nigga if it come down to it." I thought about it for a second, then said,
"I'll deal with that when the time come, but right now I need that money!"
"Alright lil nigga, here. But you ain't get that from me!"
As soon as he handed me the pistol, I felt a little rush come over me, and truthfully I liked it. I felt kinda powerful holdin' the chrome snub nosed .38 in my hand. I walked back over to where

RESPECT REVENGE Pt. 1
"When Naptown Couldn't Sleep"

Lil Smurf was standing, holding my spot as the lookout. Then I told him what I planned to do.

"Check this out Lil Smurf, this how we gonna do it. I'm a go over and hide behind Taco's car. As soon as you see me give you the thumbs up, you yell out, "Police" real loud. When you do, they gonna scatter. When Taco run to his car like he always do, I'm a jump out and do what I do."

"Man Lil E, you act like shit gonna go so smooth. What if he don't wanna give it up?"

"I'll worry about that when the time comes, just do your part." Truthfully, I had a million butterfly's floating around in my stomach but I played cool in front of Lil Smurf so he wouldn't punk out on me or make me lose my nerve. Once he had the plan, I slipped off towards Taco's car. As I was walking over, I saw my pops in front of the bar drinkin' on a 5th of Wild Irish Rose.

He said, "What's up son, throw your old man something."
I told him, "I don't got shit right now, but I might later on."
I kept it moving to my spot. Our relationship had suffered over the last year or so, I had lost a lot of respect for him, but he was still my father and I loved him regardless. I walked up beh¬ind Taco's Buick and looked over at Lil Smurf, who was across the street from where I was crouching behind the car. I flashed him the thumbs up sign, then ducked down. I was sweating bullets by then, I even thought about backing out, but I'd sold too many wolf tickets to turn back now. That wasn't even an option. Just then I heard Lil Smurf's voice,

"Police, 5-0, here they come!"

I looked up and niggas was scattering, running every which way. Just as planned, Taco was heading straight towards his car. When he finally made it over to the driver's door, I came out from behind the car wit the thirty eight in hand.

RESPECT REVENGE Pt. 1
"When Naptown Couldn't Sleep"

"Let me get it Taco! You know what it is!"
"Let you get what lil nigga?" I cocked the hammer back and said, **"Everything!"**
I seen it in his eyes that he wanted to try me because I was a lil nigga, but I guess he thought better of it, because he went in his pocket and handed me a bankroll. Then he handed me about an ounce of weed. I was getting ready to turn and run and that's when I saw the thick gold herringbone glistening under his shirt.
"Let me get that chain too!"
"Man you got the money, you ain't getting my chain!"
I reached and grabbed it and he tried to take off running. It broke at the clasp, but it cut my hand in the process. When I saw all the blood dripping from my hand, I blanked out and just started busting, **"Boc - Boc - Boc - Boc - Boc - Boc•."** I let go of all six of 'em at his fleein' backside. It happened so fast that I didn't realize how many mufuckas' was standing around watching this shit go on. When I heard the gun clicking, I snapped back to reality and took off running up the alley. I got about half way down the alley and heard somebody running behind me, I turned around and pointed the gun like I still had bullets. Lil Smurf hit the deck immediately.
"Man it's me, you trippin!"
I said, "Man you scared the shit out of me!" Get up and come on!"
We dipped around to my pops crib and laid low for the rest of the day. Smoking weed and planning on how to make the lil paper we had work for us ....

RESPECT REVENGE Pt. 1
"When Naptown Couldn't Sleep"

CHAPTER 4

All together off of the Taco lick, I came up with $1,000 and an ounce of weed. I put the necklace up because it needed to be fixed. I split the weed with Lil Smurf and then told him what I planned to do with the money.

"Both of us can go get some shoes and a couple of outfits, pay Lil Dave for this gun, cop some work from Big June, and never look back."

The talks I had been having with Lil Dave had me ready to get it.

"Man Lil E, I don't know how to sell no dope."

I said, "It can't be too hard, I stand up on that corner and watch them dudes do it all day. Plus, lil Dave said that good dope will sell itself, we just got to maintain it. You just follow my lead and watch my back and we will come up together." Lil Smurf seemed to see things my way after my lil spill, then he said,

"I got your back no matter what."

The next morning, we went out and stole us a car to get around in for the day. We hit up the mall and grabbed a few necessary things. We grabbed some all black, mid cut,

RESPECT REVENGE Pt. 1
"When Naptown Couldn't Sleep"

Reebok Classics, two pair of dickies, and two hoody sweatshirts apiece. We left the mall feeling official, neither of us had been in anything new in a long time, and it felt good. Next stop, Big June's crib. We pulled up down the street from Big June's spot and left the hot car there and walked to the house. I knocked on the door and he opened it so fast, he kinda scared me.

"What's up lil Gangsta?"
"What's up Big June, I need to holla at you about something."
"Ya'll come on in, but take ya'll shoes off at the door."
When we got into the front room, I could see why he wanted us to take our shoes off. The nigga had laid fresh white carpet all through the house. He was doing some remodeling and the furniture was all in the back of the house. Big June got Lil Smurf situated in the back room with the video game and a blunt, then took me into the kitchen. I guess when we knocked, he had been bagging up some work because there was cocaine everywhere. When I seen all the dope my eyes lit up.

"How much can you make off of all that O.G.?"

He said, "That's a half a brick right there, and it depends on how I sell it. If I sell it in ounces, I can make about $16,000 cause each ounce go for like $900.00 apiece. But if I break it down and sell rocks, I can make like $36,000 because I can bag up like $2,000 per ounce. Dig, why you want to know so much about this dope, I already hear you came up off Taco's lame ass yesterday. Plus, you and your man walk up in here all fresh and shit."

"I need to know about the dope because I'm trying to make sure I don't ever be broke again. You know my pops can't do shit for me, so I got to figure out how to do for myself."
"I feel you on that lil homie, and I'm gonna assist you in any way I can. Sit down and let me show you some shit that will take you a long way in this game."

RESPECT REVENGE Pt. 1
"When Naptown Couldn't Sleep"

He sat me down that day and showed me how to work a digital scale. He taught me how to weigh everything from an eight ball to an ounce. He taught me how to cook powder cocaine into crack, then break it down and bag it up for sell on the block. We was at it for about three or four hours straight. Lil Smurf was busy playing the game in the back room, but the only game I was interested in was the game Big June was dropping on me. By the time I left, I had soaked up so much game that I was definitely ready to put it to use. Big June sold me a half an ounce and gave me a box of baggies to get me started. Me and Lil Smurf slid back around to my crib and locked ourselves in my room to bag up the rocks and get ready to hit the block.

Big June told me to bag up all dime rocks to sell on the corner, because the fiends up there were always short of the twenty dollars that they needed to get right. So if I made my dimes fat enough to pass as twenty rocks, every time they came with thirteen or fourteen dollars, I would be the one getting over. Plus, they wouldn't complain because good dope will make a mufucka' overlook the size. So off of the 14 grams he sold me, I bagged up $ 1,000 dollars' worth of dimes. I hid the dope under all of the dirty clothes in my room, took out twenty bags, and me and Lil Smurf hit the block immediately.

The first night was a struggle. We only made $150.00, but learned a couple of valuable lessons. One was, always get the money first. Two different people saw me as a lil nigga and got my dope and took off running with it, without giving me shit. Lil Smurf had the strap, but it wasn't worth shooting nobody over twenty or thirty dollars.

The next night was a lil better. I found out what Big June meant when he said, "Good dope will sell itself." As soon as we hit the block, the smokers was on us.

"What's up lil man, you still got that same butter?"

RESPECT REVENGE Pt. 1
"When Naptown Couldn't Sleep"

"Yeah, what's up'!"
"Well let me get thirty. "
 Then the next one said, "Young blood, you still holdin' that same flavor?"
"Yeah, what you trying to do?"
"Let met me spend this twenty-five with you."
I was a natural at this hustlin' shit and it felt good. Then this chic named Felicia came through and said she didn't have no money. I told her I wasn't doing no credit.
She said, "I ain't trying to get no credit, but I will suck both of ya'll's dick for a couple of them bags."
 At first I didn't know what to say, but I had never had no head. So I found my voice and said,
"Where we gonna do it at?"
 She said, "We can go in the basement of the apartment building."
There was an abandoned 16-unit apartment building down the street that all the junkies and smokers used to get high in, and evidently anything else they needed to do. So we all walked down to the building and slid into the back and down to the basement. She told me to give her the dope first, and she tucked it into her bra, then roughly undone my belt and dropped down and had my lil joint in her mouth before I even knew what happened. I ain't never felt no shit like that in my life. I wasn't no virgin, I had slipped into a couple of the lil chicks around the way's panties when we skipped school, but once I felt the warmth and the wetness of her mouth, I knew that I would be back for more of this here. She had me weak in the knees in five minutes flat. I was still pulling my pants up and already thinking about the next time. She took care of Lil Smurf and then dipped off deep into the building, leaving us to show ourselves out. We walked back down to the strip in total silence. There wasn't much to say after that. I

RESPECT REVENGE Pt. 1
"When Naptown Couldn't Sleep"

guess what's understood need not be explained.
    The block had slowed down and I could tell Lil Smurf was getting bored. Plus, I think Felicia had made him a lil tired, so he said,
    " Man Lil E, I'm outta here. I'm headed to the crib, I'm a holla at you tomorrow."
"Alright then, give me the pistol, I'm a stay out here for a while." After he gave me the pistol I handed him fifty dollars and he was out. I was kinda disappointed in my lil partner because he didn't want no money. He was satisfied with the fifty dollars I gave him. I stayed out there a couple of more hours and made several more trips to the stash spot. It took me three days to finish the first sack that I copped from Big June, and after that I started copping at least twice a week. Even taking the losses I was taking learning the game, I got the hang of flipping the dope and managing my money within the first six months. Most of my losses came from fucking with my pops, if I wasn't giving him something, he was stealing it or runnin' off with it.
    It had been eight months since I'd robbed Taco and I was now a fixture on the corner. I was taking care of my business. I paid the utilities around my pops crib, we had lights, water and gas. I had gear and I kept on fresh kicks. Plus, all the lil hood rats was checking for a nigga. So shit was all good for ya boy. That is until one morning in the spring of "93". I had just come out of the variety store on the corner, I
had bought me an orange juice and a blunt to get my day going. I came out talking to another young hustler from the hood, when I saw Taco's Buick sitting at the curb. As soon as I seen it I started to leave, but I thought; I can't duck this nigga forever so I might as well face him, just to see what it do. The homie Lil Dave walked up and said,

RESPECT REVENGE Pt. 1
"When Naptown Couldn't Sleep"

"I hope you strapped cause Taco is in the barber shop and he just asked about you a minute ago."

"Yeah I'm strapped and I'm a be out here when he come out."

Lil Dave said, "Aight then, I'm a holla back."

Then he walked off. About five minutes later, I had come off the side of the building after serving one of my fiends and Taco walked right into my path. The nigga tried to look tough, but I had caught him off guard and he was just as shook as I was.

He said, "What's up lil dude?"

I said, "What's up with you?"

This nigga balled up his fist like he was getting ready to fight or something. This cat was way older and way bigger than me and I knew that I couldn't whoop him so I up'd that thang on his ass.

"Nigga get in your car and get off this block and never come back."

He looked me in the eye and said, "You lil bitch ass nigga, who the fuck you think you are. I been coming round here before you could even come off the porch. What I look like lettin' a bitch…"

Before he could even finish trying to convince himself, I popped him in both legs. **Boc! Boc!** The nigga hit the ground like dead weight. I don't even remember what I was thinking, all I remember was the two noises. The bang of the gun, and him screaming like the bitch that he had just called me. What I do remember was the feeling of power that I felt, as I watched him squirming around trying to hold both legs at one time. This nigga was way bigger, faster and stronger than me. Yet this gun had equalized all that. I knew right then that I would have one on me at all times….

RESPECT REVENGE Pt. 1
"When Naptown Couldn't Sleep"

CHAPTER 5

Word around the hood spread quickly about me shootin' Taco. Everybody knew it, even the damn police. The nigga told on me on the way to the hospital. The police was sweating the block for the rest of the day looking for me. But after that, they wasn't kicking down doors or nothing. To them, it wasn't nothing but more black on black crime, and not worth the time and effort to keep looking for me. Now everybody in the Hard-Part, both young and old knew a nigga name and showed me love, like I had graduated high school or something. I guess on some hood shit, I had graduated, from a lil dude in the hood, to a "Bottom Boy." I stopped playing the block so hard in the day time, so I wouldn't get picked up on a hum-bug. I mainly just started grinding at night. That night shift was crazy, that's when the block really came alive. Lil Smurf really wasn't with the all night hustlin, so we kinda drifted apart as far as hanging went. What I did do was give him enough work to last him through the day, and picked up the money from him when he was done. I had started hanging wit these two stick up boys. "P.U." and "Lil Lucky." They stole cars and went around robbing

RESPECT REVENGE Pt. 1
"When Naptown Couldn't Sleep"

corner boys from other hoods. If you weren't plugged in with Big June, you could be from the Hard-Part and still become a victim. The name of the Hood was the "Hard-Part", but Big June had named all the young rowdy mufuckas' who loved that pistol play, the "Bottom Boys." Being that the Bottom Boys knew that I would bust my gun, they started lettin' a nigga hang with them on the late nights. I even went on a couple of licks with em'. We was like vampires, from sun up to sun down, we was at it. At the first sign of light, everyone went and laid it down to get ready for the next night.

  The block was particularly hot one night and mostly everybody had cut out early because the police were everywhere. Me being greedy, trying to get that money, I stayed out there doing my thang. I was serving one of my regular customers when the police jumped out of a grey minivan and caught me slippin'. They didn't find my dope because the fiend I was serving told me to give her the work and she swallowed it. But they did catch me with the burner. I sat in the back of the police car while he did the paper work, just knowing I was hit. Somebody in the hood went and found my father and told him what was up. He walked up and asked the officer,

"What ya'll got him for? I'm his father."

The police answered, "He has a warrant for an aggravated battery, plus I got him for a weapons violation and curfew."

My pops tried to come to my defense. "He was out here wit' me." "Well if he was with you, then you must of known he had this gun and if that's the case, then I got to lock both of ya'll up!" With that, my pops got little, he didn't want to go to jail for no bull-shit, so he left it at that.

  They took me to the juvenile detention center and processed me in. I laid in this lil holding tank until the wee hours

RESPECT REVENGE Pt. 1
"When Naptown Couldn't Sleep"

of the morning. Once I was fed and clothed, I was sent to a unit with dudes my own age. I couldn't go to court until Monday morning because I had been arrested on a Friday night, so I was hit for the weekend. When I told the dudes that were in my unit that I was from the Hard-Part and that I was a Bottom Boy, I realized how much weight the name held around the city. At first, niggas had they mug on mean and was acting like they might want to try a nigga. They changed their whole demeanor once I let em' know that I repped the Hard-Part.

Monday morning rolled around and I was called out early for an attorney visit. I walked in this little meeting room and shook the hand of a pretty, dark skinned woman, with long, jet black hair. She had a friendly smile and she made me feel comfortable immediately.

"Hi Mr. Hunt, I'm LaTanya Williams and I will be representing you in these matters. Do you have any questions or concerns for me, or anything at all that you would like to ask me?"

I said, "How much time am I facing, and will I be able to go home today?"

"Well, this is not the adult system and things work a little differently here. The judge has a lot of discretion on how to hand out sentences to juvenile offenders. If she feels that you only need a little help to get yourself back on track, then she could give you as little as three to six months. On the other hand, if she feels that you are a danger or a threat to society, then you could receive anything from now, until the day before your twenty first birthday. So tell me what happened and we will see what our best course of action will be."

I told her that this grown man had tried to put his hands on me and I ran the first time. The next time he tried it, I pulled out a gun and shot him in both legs.

RESPECT REVENGE Pt. 1
"When Naptown Couldn't Sleep"

She asked me, "Where did you get the gun?"
"Found it in an alley in my neighborhood."
"Look Eric, I have talked to your grandmother and she told me about the problems that you been having with your dad and his drug problems. I know you have had it rough, but the only way that I can help you is if you be honest with me."
"I am being honest with you. You said you talked to my granny, where she at?"
"Her and you Auntie Rhonda are out there in the waiting room; they will be in court with you today. I'm going to let you speak to them for a moment, to let them help you decide what's best for you, then I'll see you in court in a half an hour."

She walked out of the room, leaving me alone for a few minutes, while she went to get my folks. A few minutes later, a deputy let my granny and auntie into the room. I stood up and gave them both a hug, first my auntie and then my granny. My granny said,
"Hey baby, how you holding up in here?"
I hugged her and tried to be solid, but I could feel all the pent up emotions coming to the surface. I tried to talk but no words came out, I just started crying and letting the tears flow. She rubbed my back as we hugged and said,
"It's okay baby, let it out, everything is gonna be alright."
Then my Auntie Rhonda got in on the hugging and we all were standing in the middle of the floor crying a river. When we finally sat down, auntie said,
"So what are you going to tell the judge baby? Are you gonna admit or deny the charges?"
I asked her what she thought I should do.
"Did you shoot him?"
"Yeah I shot him, he was getting ready to put his hands on me and I was scared."

RESPECT REVENGE Pt. 1
"When Naptown Couldn't Sleep"

"What did you do to him, or was he just looking for a fight?"
"I didn't do nothing to him auntie, he was just trippin'."
My granny had just sat back and took it all in, then she spoke up.
"Well if you ain't done nothing, then why was you just walking around with a gun?"
I looked at her and was getting ready to tell another lie, then couldn't even do it. I just put my head down on the table and she kept on,
"Listen baby, I done heard a few things bout you out there on Harding. They say you out there hustling and up and down the block all times of the night. I know you are out there on the devil's playground and a lot of foolishness comes with them streets. Now you know you are my baby, and I'm with you rather you are right or wrong, but sometimes when you have done a lil wrong, the best thing to do to fix it is what's right. So I'm a let you think on that for a minute and decide what you want to do. I'll be there for you regardless of what you decide."
My auntie had been holding my hand the whole time. She leaned in and kissed my face and said,
"When this is all over you are coming back to live with us."
My granny got up and hugged me tight then told me that she loved me, then knocked on the door for the deputy to let them out. The things my granny had said weighed heavily on my mind. I figured if I was going to go away for a lil while, then I may as well go ahead and get it over with as soon as possible.
    I stepped in the courtroom and noticed my granny and auntie sitting in the front row, right behind where my public defender was seated. I looked around to see if my father had bothered to show, and I spotted him in the last row. He looked bad, you could tell that he had been up doing his thang all weekend long. He gave me a little nod and I returned it, then I

RESPECT REVENGE Pt. 1
"When Naptown Couldn't Sleep"

stood in front of the judge.

 The judge was a mean looking old white broad. I don't even remember her name, but she gave me the impression of someone who wasn't to be played with. She read me a bunch of legal mumbo jumbo, that all boiled down to me being able to plead not guilty and have a bench trial. Where I would be able to dispute or counter any and all evidence that the state brought against me. Then she informed me that I could waive those rights and admit my fault today, and allow her to impose a sanction here and now. I had talked it over with my attorney and we decided that I would come out better if I admit my wrongs and ask for mercy. My lawyer told the judge my intentions of waiving my rights and gave her a brief summary of my family history. She painted a very ugly picture of my father and his parenting skills. I had never heard anyone talk about my living situation and conditions out loud, and hearing another person speak on it made it sound worse than what I thought it was. The judge spoke up and asked me was my father here in the courtroom today.

 I said, "No ma'am he could not make it today because he is sick."

I don't know why I felt the need to cover for him, but I knew he would not want to stand here in front of all these people and lay all his cards on the table. So I saw no reason for him to have to. The judge asked me to give her a brief summary of what had taken place and I stuck to the same story that I had given my lawyer. Then the judge said,

 "You are a young man who has seen too much in your young life. I do believe that you are a victim of your own circumstances or those of your father. I can also tell that you're loyal to him because I have seen many young people in here that will try to use any advantage they can to gain favor from the court. You, on the other hand, took the blame for your own

RESPECT REVENGE Pt. 1
"When Naptown Couldn't Sleep"

actions and didn't try and blame your father for what you did yourself. For that I commend you. However, you did shoot an unarmed man, not once, but twice. Then you got caught with a firearm. So you need correction for your actions. So, with that said, I hereby commit you to the youth authority, also known as Boy School, for a term of twelve to eighteen months. Good luck Mr. Hunt."

RESPECT REVENGE Pt. 1
"When Naptown Couldn't Sleep"

CHAPTER 6

I ended up at a juvenile facility for violent offenders that was about an hour outside of the city. The place itself wasn't that bad, but the inmate population was off the chain. They had real good education programs, good recreation, with a nice weight pile and even the food wasn't bad. But it was non-stop action amongst the gangs and races. Every thirty minutes you would hear, "Code Blue! Code Blue in the mess hall!" and the guards would be running to break up a fight. Then, "Code Blue in the gymnasium!" and they would be running again. They kept the guards busy all day long. I had hooked up with a couple of young niggas from the Westside of my city and we pretty much just did us. We had a routine that we did every day. Get up, go to breakfast, then to G.E.D. class from 8-11 a.m., then go to lunch. From 1- 2 p.m., we played basketball in the gym. Then from 2-3 p.m., we was on the weight pile. After that we ate dinner, then I would go to my room and read or just think for the rest of the day. All kinds of thoughts passed through my mind. I thought about how me robbing and shooting Taco, had gotten me respected in the hood. I thought about how the O.G. of the hood, Big

RESPECT REVENGE Pt. 1
"When Naptown Couldn't Sleep"

June fucked wit me and had sat me down and showed me how to get money. Then I would think about just how much money I could have been getting out there. My mind was made up, when I touched down, I would be on a mission to get money. I'd had a taste of it, and everybody knows that when you taste something good, it only makes you hungry for more and I was definitely hungry for my fair share.

My time flew by so fast sticking to my little routine, that I looked up and was only one month from the door. It was April of "94" and I was due to be released in May. My granny, Auntie, and Keisha had come to visit me every other weekend the whole time I was there. They had brought me clothes and shoes for when I got out and had set me up back in my old room in granny's house. Auntie Rhonda and Keisha had moved into their own house further out East in an area of the city known as "Brightwood", so it would be just me and granny in the crib. Those were the only people that I really cared about in the world, outside of pops' and the day I was released, they were at the gates waiting on me.

Keisha jumped out of the car and ran over to hug me. She threw her arms around my neck and kissed me all over my face,
"Hey big cuz, I know you glad to be out there!"
"Hell yeah I'm glad, plus I need to be out here to keep yo fast ass in check!"
"Boy please, you don't got to worry about me, I ain't messing wit no boys."
Keisha was 13 going on 30. Granny had already told me how she stayed on the phone all times of the night talking to these lil boys. Some times until she fell asleep with the phone still up to her ear. She was a spitting image of Auntie Rhonda and was developing fast. I was going to have my hands full out there because I wasn't

RESPECT REVENGE Pt. 1
"When Naptown Couldn't Sleep"

getting ready to let none of these lil knuckle heads have they way with or hurt my baby cousin. Auntie and granny had made their way over to us and granny said,

"Come here baby, give your granny some love."

Me and granny hugged like we hadn't seen each other in years.

"I'm glad to have you home baby."

"I'm glad to be home granny."

Auntie said, "Dang momma, let the boy go so he can give his auntie some of that sugar."

She held me at arm's length and said,

"Boy you done got so big, looking like a grown man. You look just like yo' daddy when he was yo' age."

For the year I had been down, I had hit the weights constantly and if you add that with the growth spurt I'd had, I was a big boy. I was only 16 and was 5"11 and 185 pounds. Plus, the weights had ripped me up kinda decent. I had let my hair grow out and rocked it in six french braids to the back. Add that with my light brown skin and I wasn't hard to look at, if I must say so myself. Auntie pulled me in and hugged me tight, then slid me three crispy, new, one hundred dollar bills.

"It ain't much but it will hold you until you find yourself a job."

"Thanks Auntie, I appreciate it."

Auntie had come up a lil bit, she owned a lil clothing boutique that sold strictly designer labels and she was making good money. She made sure she took care of her loved ones. I guess clubbing all those years, gave her a taste for fashion and she was making it work for her. We all got in her "92" Nissan Maxima and headed towards granny's crib.

Granny had cooked a big boy soul food meal to celebrate a niggas' homecoming. She had fried chicken, mashed potatoes, mac and cheese, potato salad, collard greens, dinner roll's, and of

RESPECT REVENGE Pt. 1
"When Naptown Couldn't Sleep"

course, her famous homemade peach cobbler. We all sat around the table eating and talking, just catching up on what's been going on. They were doing most of the talkin', I was hunched over my plate trying to kill myself with my first home cooked meal in over a year. Keisha cut right into me,

"Dang Eric, you act like your food gonna get up and run!" Granny came to my defense quick,
"Shut up girl and leave my boy alone and let him eat, he ain't had his granny's cooking in a while, ain't that right baby?" I answered with a smile,
"That's right granny, get her up off my back. Ain't nothing changed around here Keisha, I'm still the man round here."
We all had a laugh and the mood turned kinda serious.

"So, where my daddy at granny? Have you heard from him?"

"He was by here the other day, begging to cut my grass for $30. I just gave him $20 and sent him on his way. He looks worse and worse every time I see him. It breaks my heart to see my boy out there like that. He be lying, talking bout he done quit getting high and he been looking for a job. That boy ain't filled out nobody's application." Auntie Rhonda cut right in.

"I be letting him work up at the shop on the weekends to try and keep him off the streets, but as soon as I give him his lil pay, he be gone. That is my brother and I love him to death, but he gone. The only thing that can save him is God, and if God don't get him soon, the grave will."
Keisha had already crept off and was busy runnin' her mouth on the phone in the front room. Granny and Auntie started to clean up, so I eased up on Keisha.

"Girl who you talking to on that phone?"
"My friend why?"
"Don't be asking me why, you gonna make me hurt one of them

RESPECT REVENGE Pt. 1
"When Naptown Couldn't Sleep"

lil niggas' bout you, watch!"
"You ain't gonna have to do that, cause I ain't doing nothing but talking."
"You better not be!" And I left it at that.
I chilled with granny for the next two months. I was working at Auntie's boutique every day because I wasn't in school. I had gotten my G.E.D. during my lil vacation and she was giving me $200 a week just to keep the place clean, wipe down the windows and keeping the grass cut. She was trying to keep me out of the streets, but it wasn't nothing she could do, it was already in me.

I got off my little job at the shop one Friday night and was getting ready to hit the hood for the first time since I had been out. Granny came to my door and said,
"Before you leave, come talk to me for a minute."
My granny was only 56 years old, but had been around for many moons, so wisdom wasn't where she was lacking. My granny been in church heavy since she was thirty-five and ain't had a drink or a smoke since. So the granny I know has always been saved and sanctified. Before my time though, it was a different story.

When I walked in her room, she had this very concerned look on her face. Granny is my heart, so I was concerned immediately about what had her so serious. She sat me down on her bed, and she sat in her favorite chair directly across from me and then said,

"Listen baby, I'm your grandmother and I love you with all my heart. I've had you in my home since you were a baby and raised you as my own. You are my first grandchild, but I'm closer to you than I am to my own children, we just bonded. I've watched you grow from a boy to a young man. Now that you are getting older, your decisions have a more direct effect on the outcome of your life. I know you have been hurting on the inside because of your father, but baby you have got to start thinking

RESPECT REVENGE Pt. 1
"When Naptown Couldn't Sleep"

about yourself. You were exposed to the streets because of the actions of your father, and I can see by your words and actions that you are going back out there to try and live the street life. It's in your system now, but it always been in your blood. Your father's father was a street person. He is what ran me to God. He ran the streets and sold drugs, shot craps and everything else that you can think of that's associated with them streets. He use to come home all types of hours, if he even came home at all. We split up from the time your father was seven until he was seventeen. I still kept track of what he got into in them streets and he stayed in some mess. Shootings, and robberies, he even got stabbed six times in a dice game, over a five-dollar bet. Then he came sniffing around and the love I had for him made me take him back after ten long years. He had slowed down a little bit and was just making his lil money and coming home. Then he started drinking real heavy. He would come home talking all loud and acting like he wanted to fight, then just end up passing out somewhere. Well one night he didn't come home at all and I got beside myself and went out looking for him. I went through his usual hangouts and nobody had seen him, so I called his brother and asked him had he seen him. He said that he was over there asleep on his couch. I go over there and he is knocked out cold. I woke him up and he was acting all strange and nervous."

    He sat up and looked at me all hazy eyed, and said, "Baby what you doing here?"
I said, "I'm here to ask you the same question."
"I came over here because I didn't want to come home like this, I robbed this lil jidda bug earlier tonight and came over here and snorted a few lines and had a few drinks and ended up smashed. I didn't want to come home trippin' so I decided to sleep it off."
He came on home that night and everything was good for about a week. Then the next Friday came around and he said he was

RESPECT REVENGE Pt. 1
"When Naptown Couldn't Sleep"

going out for a while and he would be back. I begged him not to go because I had a bad feeling in my gut, like a woman's intuition. He told me I was trippin' and he would be back in a few hours. I gave up arguing and went on and laid down for the night. I had been sleep for a couple of hours, when I heard some gun shots. It wasn't all that unusual to hear em' so I laid back down. Five minutes later, my next door neighbor came bangin' on my door talking bout,

"Stevie been shot! He out back!"

I got up and ran out back and sure enough it's him. He was bleeding real bad and having trouble breathing. Well, they hauls him off to the hospital and he didn't make it. You talking bout hurting, I loved that man with all of my soul. It turned out that the little jidda bug he had robbed the week before, never got over it and came looking for him and caught him coming through the alley on his way home and killed him.

"Baby, the reason I'm telling you this is because them streets are for real and they play for keeps. I don't want you out there, God knows I don't, but I can see it in your eyes that you are going out there anyway. So I'm telling you, don't go out there half steppin'. I couldn't stand for nothing to happen to you out there, that would break my heart. Don't ever under estimate anyone and don't let nobody do nothin' to you, you hear me?"

I let the things that she had said sink in, I realized that she was speaking about Taco, and me shooting him. This was the first of its kind, but over the years, granny would become somewhat of a counselor to me. She had jewels to drop and she always dropped them on me at the right time. With that, it was time for me to hit the hood.

RESPECT REVENGE Pt. 1
"When Naptown Couldn't Sleep"

CHAPTER 7
Summer of "94"

It felt good being back in the Hard-Part. I remember the first time I saw the hood when we moved over here in "89". It was something that I wasn't use to, but now I felt like this was my element. From the looks of things, shit was still moving and shaking. It was Friday evening and the block was definitely in full swing. I noticed a few of my old customers coming and going, trying to copp this or sell that. That's one thing about the hood, it was better than the Home Shopping Network. You could pretty much buy anything you needed right there on the curb. You didn't even need no credit card or cash. The currency that made shit move out here was "crack cocaine." With a crack sack, you can buy pussy, rent a car, trade it for a major household appliance, or just trade it for whatever your drug of choice is. If a crackhead knows you will trade him some crack for it, there is nothing they can't get you. I stopped this old head named Ronnie that I use to deal with.

"What's up Ronnie, what you trying to do with that V.C.R.?"
"You know me nephew, I'm trying to get something proper

RESPECT REVENGE Pt. 1
"When Naptown Couldn't Sleep"

for this here, throw me a fifty and you can have this mufucka!"
"Naw I'm straight right now, but if I had some work, I would take that off your hands."
He said, "Boy I can tell you been on one of them special vacations, you look like you was lifting every weight in the jail."
"I was doin' a lil sumthin'. What's up wit Lil Smurf, you seen him around?"
I seen the lil nigga' earlier today round on 26th Street. I got his pager number if you want it."
"Naw I'm cool, I'll run into him somewhere out here."
He said, "A'ight young blood, I'll holla at you later, I got to get rid of this merch so I can get right."
I leaned on the wall in front of the variety store on the corner and just watched the comings and goings for a minute. I had been out there for maybe ten or fifteen minutes and my old man bent the corner, walking with some new young nigga on the block. I could tell he had just copped something cause he was steppin' kinda fast, like he was on a mission. I called him.
"Hey Daddy! Hey Pops!"
He didn't even break his stride. So I tried his real name,
"Big Ed!"
He turned his head around and looked my way. When he finally realized it was me, he damn near ran to me.
"What's up my guy? When you get out?!"
"I been out for a couple months now. I been laying low over Granny crib trying to get my head right. What's been up wit' you?"
"Aw man, I been just chillin', trying to slow my roll a lil bit."
Pops was looking bad, he didn't even look like himself anymore, but he was grown and I loved him regardless. I didn't see no since in trying to preach to him and tell him shit I know he had heard a

RESPECT REVENGE Pt. 1
"When Naptown Couldn't Sleep"

thousand times over. He changed the subject.

"Man look at you, you damn near tall as me, all bulky and shit. That year done turned you into a man huh? Wait till' I tell Big June my boy out. That nigga love you, he ask me about you all the time."

"Yeah, if you see him, tell him I'll be at him later on okay."

"So where you staying at son?"

"I still got my room at granny's crib, but I'm a be in the hood somewhere."

"You can come on around to the house if you need to."

"I might swing on around there and check you out."

"A'ight then son. I love you okay."

"Yeah I know; I love you too."

We hugged for a second, and he was out. As I watched him slip off down the alley, I thought about all he used to be, compared to what he was now. That crack was a bad bitch. As I was deep in thought thinking about my father, I was snapped back by a familiar voice coming from the side of the building arguing with somebody.

"Man fuck you! I ain't sold you no shit like that! You better get that dope fiend shit on out of here!" Then the other voice said, "I ain't even went nowhere! I went right around back to smoke this shit and it's soap!"

"Man, I ain't sold you no soap! Now get on before you get spit on!"

"Lil Smurf. I ought to .... "

"You ought to what?"

I cut him off before he could even finish. They both turned around and looked at me. Lil Smurf's face lit up and he ran over to me.

RESPECT REVENGE Pt. 1
"When Naptown Couldn't Sleep"

"Man Lil E, when you get out nigga? I'm glad to see yo crazy ass. That nigga Taco got a permanent limp, and every time I see him, I think about yo ass."
By then the base head had realized he was beat, so he slumped his shoulders and started to walk away. I hollered at him,
"Hey my man, don't trip, we gonna straighten that out later on a'ight?"
"A'ight youngin', I'm a hold you to that."
Me and Lil Smurf walked back around to the front and went in the variety store.
I said, "Lil Smurf, you still up to your same stunts huh?"
"Naw, I just been hittin' bad lately and needed a few dollars, so I burned him, but I ain't been on that shit like that."
Old man Doc, who owned the variety store, was an old hustler from way back. He owned a lot of houses in the hood, plus the building that held his store, the barbershop, and a lil pizza place. He was in tune with everything that went on out here. When he saw, me he took no time gettin' at me.
"What's up Lil E, when they let you lose baby?"
"I been out a couple of months now, just been laying back. How you been Doc?"
"Old man ain't raisin' no hell. I'm glad to see you home youngin'. Here hold on to this until you see better days."
He pushed a fresh C-note into my palm and gave me a wink.
"Good lookin' Doc, I appreciate that man."
"Don't mention it. Hey E, keep your head up out here man."
"A'ight old school."
Doc was a good dude, I respected him.
Lil Smurf walked up to the counter and said,
"Let me get a pack of Newport Kings in the soft pack, and two Swisher Sweets Doc."
"That will be$ 4.50 shorty."

RESPECT REVENGE Pt. 1
"When Naptown Couldn't Sleep"

Smurf paid for the goods and we was out.
    We headed around to 26th Street, where Lil Smurf lived with hi moms'. They had a two-bedroom flat that had seen better days, but Ms. Ann kept it clean.
 Ms. Ann said, "Lil Smurf, who the hell is that you done brought up in my house?"
 "Momma, that's Lil E. My man back home now."
"Damn! That is Lil E. Boy, you done got big as hell. When you get out of there?"
If I had to answer that question one more time, I might die.
"I been out for a couple of months now Ms. Ann."
"Well come on over here and give Ms. Ann a hug!"
I stepped forward to show Ms. Ann some love and all I smelled was Wild Irish Rose. You would have thought she took a bath in the stuff, but that was what Ms. Ann. drunk from sun up to sun down. She was good people though, just loud as hell and cursed like a sailor.
    Lil Smurf said, "Momma, we gonna be on the porch a'ight?"
"Yeah, but give me five dollars before you go."
"Ma, I ain't got no money."
"Boy give me five dollars before I cuss yo ass out! Always talking bout what you ain't got! What you ain't got is good got damn sense!"
He gave up the five spot in a hurry after that to calm her down. Because once she got going, it wouldn't be no stopping her. I just laughed, cause it felt good to be back in the hood.
We sat on milk crates on the porch and twisted up a couple of blunts, while Lil Smurf caught me up on what had been going on in the hood. He said that Lil Dave was locked up. Dave was Big Junes' right hand man. The one who gave me the pistol to rob Taco. Him being locked up explained why I saw all the new faces

RESPECT REVENGE Pt. 1
"When Naptown Couldn't Sleep"

up on the corner. He said Big June was still doing his thang', but he was moving through this cat named Money now. Money had came home from the Feds' about six months ago. Just as he was tellin' me this, this lil thick redbone came out on the porch next door and yelled,

"Sean! Get in here, momma want you!"

I said, "Smurf who dat?"

"That's big head ass Trasheen, everybody calls her Sheen though. She ain't giving up no pussy, that bitch think she all that, she just want to smoke a nigga' weed up."

She must have felt us talkin' bout her, cause she looked right over and said,

"Let me hit that Lil Smurf?"

"Hit what, this is a square!"

"Boy boo! I know that "Gangsta" when I smell it."

"Naw, you can't hit this, this is my niggas' welcome home sack."

"Welcome home from where?"

She came off her porch and came over onto Lil Smurf's. Now I could see her good. Baby girl was right. Fat lil titties, nice plump lil ass, pretty light skin, plus had that hood attitude to go wit it. I spoke up,

"My name Lil E, and yeah you can hit the weed."

Lil Smurf looked up at me like I had lost my mind, but passed her the blunt anyway. She took a hit of the blunt and looked me up and down.

"Where you just get out from?"

"I just got out of boy school."

"How long you been gone?"

"12 months, 2 weeks, and 3 days."

"Damn, you got that down packed huh?"

"You would too if you had been couped up that long."

RESPECT REVENGE Pt. 1
"When Naptown Couldn't Sleep"

She handed me the blunt and gave me this real cute lil look. Smurf peeped game and let her sit down.
"Im a go in here and check on momma and let ya'll talk for a minute."
 I could tell baby girl was feelin' a nigga', she was all smiles. She said,
    "Who been doin' yo hair?"
    "My lil cousin hit me up, why?"
"Because I can do better that's why. I'm the tightest around here, you better ask somebody."
    "Girl how old are you?"
    "I'm 16 ½, I'll be 17 in December. How old are you?"
    "I'll be 17 next month."
    She smiled and said, "So what, you ain't grown."
I laughed at that, baby girl was a handful. Plus, I hadn't had no pussy in 15 months and she was lookin' right. So I asked her,
    "Who over yo house?"
"My momma over there, but she a be sleep pretty soon, she drunk."
    I said, "So, when can I come and get my hair done?"
    "When you want to?"
"I guess about a hour or so, I'll be finished with what I got to do. Is that too late?"
    "Just call me and see if I'm still up."
She took out a pen and wrote her number on my hand, smiled at a nigga', and walked back over to her house, switching that fat lil ass the whole way.
Lil Smurf had to be ease dropping the whole time because he came right out.
    "Man she ain't gonna let you hit it, you wasting yo time. I been tryin' to fuck all summer long."
He sounded convinced, but I had a feelin' that she was gonna let

RESPECT REVENGE Pt. 1
"When Naptown Couldn't Sleep"

a nigga get these nuts out of pawn, my shit had been on the shelf for too long.

I chilled wit my lil partner for about another 30 or 45 minutes, then it was time to roll out.

"I'm out Lil Smurf, I'm a hit you tomorrow."

"Where you goin' my nigga?"

"I'm bout to slide around to Big Junes' crib, then probably to my pops spot."

"What you going to do around there? That's a bonafide crack house now, if you need a place to crash, just come on back through. You can come down the basement with me, just tap on the window."

"A'ight then I'm a holla back."

It was 9:00p.m. by then and I wanted to catch Big June before it got late. I slid out the back way from Lil Smurf's and headed down the alley towards the Big Homies crib. If I was going to get on my feet, Big June was going to be the key.

RESPECT REVENGE Pt. 1
"When Naptown Couldn't Sleep"

CHAPTER 8

"Boc! Boc! Boc!" Three fast gun shots in a row, and I ain't talking bout no lil shit either. This was .9 milli or better. I was cuttin' through the field, heading towards Big June's crib. I stopped in my tracks when I heard the shots, but when I heard the scream that sounded like a man, but could have passed for a female, I knew something was wrong. I heard footsteps coming my way, like someone was running right at me, so I dipped off in some bushes and got low. I seen these two mufuckas' chasing some old head and they were coming right towards me. The old head collapsed no more than ten feet away from where I was hiding.
        He said, "Come on man! Please! It wasn't me! Don't Kill me! Help!! Help me!!"
He was screaming at the top of his lungs.
        "Well if it wasn't you, then who was it then? Who the fuck broke in my muthafucking house? It was either you or that stealing ass nigga Randall!"
I couldn't believe what I was seeing. Big June was standing over the old head with murda written all over his face. The old head kept tryin' to save himself.

RESPECT REVENGE Pt. 1
"When Naptown Couldn't Sleep"

"It was Randall! Please, get me some help back here before I fuck around and die!"

He was in extreme pain cause he was talking through clenched teeth.

Big June said, "That's just like a disloyal mufucka, rat your partner out when a nigga put a lil heat under your ass!"

"Boc! Boc!"

Big June put two in my mans' head and silenced him for good. He looked at the nigga he was wit and said,

"Grab his legs."

Big June grabbed his arms and they tossed the nigga in the bushes right next to me, causing me to make some noise and giving up my hiding place. **"Clack Clack!** Two guns cocked at the same time.

"Who the fuck is that, you got about two seconds to come up out them bushes wit yo hands up or I'm a lay you down right there!"

"Hold up! Hold up! It's me, It's Lil E."

I came up like a jack in the box.

Big June said, "What the fuck is you doin' in the bushes?"

"Man I heard shots and heard somebody runnin' my way and I got low, I was on my way to your crib!"

"Your old man told me you was out, but I didn't expect to find you hiding in no bushes."

This whole conversation was taking place while I had two .40 cals pointed at my head. Big June turned to the cat he was with and said,

"Dig Money, gone back to my crib, I'll be around there in a minute."

Money gave him a head nod and turned and left the same way he came. I just knew, being that I had just witnessed a murder, and he sent his partner away, that Big June was getting ready to finish

RESPECT REVENGE Pt. 1
"When Naptown Couldn't Sleep"

me off and leave me back here with ol' boy. He said,
    "Put yo hands down lil nigga, I know you a thoroughbred. You ain't seen nothin' no way did you?"
"Naw I ain't seen nuttin'!"
"Good, keep it that way then. That mufucka broke in my house and he fucked up my white carpet too, and you know that's a no-no."
"Put yo hands down lil nigga, I know you a thoroughbred. You ain't seen nothin' no way did you?"
"Naw I ain't seen nuttin'!"
"Good, keep it that way then. That mufucka broke in my house and he fucked up my white carpet too, and you know that's a no-no."
When he said that we both laughed and I gave him some dap and we headed to his crib.
    Shit was way different in his house now. He had white wall to wall carpet, with big white leather furniture, and glass tables. Against the wall opposite the couch, and diagonal from the love seat, was the biggest T.V. I had ever seen. There was a big ass picture of "Scarface" wit powder all over his nose, with the words "Say goodnight to the bad guy!" written under it, hanging right behind the couch. When we walked in, all you could smell was that good smoke. I had just damn near shitted on myself in them bushes, so I needed something to calm my nerves. Me and Big June sat at the kitchen table, coincidently; the same spot where he gave me my first crack sack and the game on how to make it work for me. Big June said,
    "Hey Money! Come in here real quick and meet my nigga Lil E! He fresh home and shit!"
When Money came in the room I could now see that he wasn't no young nigga'. The darkness had hid his features, he was about 24 or 25 and brown skinned, with one of them thin wire framed

RESPECT REVENGE Pt. 1
"When Naptown Couldn't Sleep"

bodies that is stronger than it looks. He rocked his hair low all over and had a thin mustache and goatee.

Money said, "What's up Lil homie, my name Money."
I dapped him up and said, "I'm Lil E."
"Oh, you the young nigga' that set fire to Tacos' ass up on the corner a while back huh? I remember hearing bout that."

Big June cut in, "Money, Lil E is my lil man. I was grooming him before he left. I want you to take him under your wing on that corner, let him run it if you want too. He is a hustlin' young nigga, and I trust him up there."

Money answered, "A'ight then, I'm gettin' ready to roll out right now, but here go my pager number lil homie. Hit me up when you ready to rock."

"Good lookin' Money, I'm a hit you up tomorrow if that's cool?"
"Yeah, it's all good. I'm a holla at ya'll later. I'm finna go fall off in me some pussy."
With that Money was out the door.

After money bounced, Big June blazed a couple blunts of that "Gangsta" wit a nigga. He had that shit wit no seeds and had frost all over it. You had to take your time with it or you might fuck around and cough up a lung. While we smoked, he gave me the run down on everything that had been going down in the ghetto. He told me about these niggas' out of Riverside that our hood been beefin' wit. They had tried to set up shop in the hood knowing that it might be consequences and repercussions. So the Big Homie had let the Bottom Boys loose on them. The young boys had given' them all that they could handle and sent them packin' back to their own hood quick. Riverside is another hood on the Westside. They known for bein' hustlers and gettin' plenty of money, plus they bout that drama. Right before I got caught and sent off; me, Lil Lucky, and P.U. had been ridin' through

RESPECT REVENGE Pt. 1
"When Naptown Couldn't Sleep"

the hood terrorizing anybody we caught out there trying to curb serve. Once, Big June had sent Lil Lucky and P.U. at em', and ran em' up out the hood, he started runnin' up in they spots, taking all their dope. He said he was duck taping them niggas', making em' tell him where it was at. The kinda money he was talking bout was enough to have me wanting to ride wit him and get me some of that bread. Big June loved young niggas', cause he said they were more loyal and he could mold em' into real soldiers, and that is exactly what he was doin' wit me. He told me once he get the bricks, he bring them back to the hood and give em' to Money and let him push the work in the hood so everybody could eat. I knew that just by him telling me all this, he was offering me a chance to eat off of either plate. I was down for whatever it took to get on my feet and would be about my business, whatever the Big Homie had me doing. He had put a lot on my mind, and the good smoke had me thinking about how I was getting ready to find my lane and ride it all the way out. I told Big June that I was out and would be at him tomorrow. I needed to go somewhere and relax my mind and get ready to make it do what it do.

RESPECT REVENGE Pt. 1
"When Naptown Couldn't Sleep"

CHAPTER 9

I ended up going back around Lil Smurf's crib after I left the Big Homies spot. I was fucked up from all the smoking, and needed to lay it down. I got up the next morning and sat on the front porch and was smoking a Newport, when I heard, "Damn, I must have scared you or something. I thought you was coming over to get your hair done last night."
 It was Trasheen looking all good early in the morning.
I said, "Naw it wasn't that, I got caught up last night and couldn't make it back. But what's up, can you do it now?"
"Yeah, my momma gone right now, so come on."
I got up and went over to her porch.
"Yo momma ain't gonna come home trippin' is she?"
"Naw she won't be back until 4 or 5:00, so we good!"
She took me up in her room and told me to take my hair down, while she ran down stairs real quick. I sat down on her bed, which was way down on the floor. Just a queen sized mattress and boxspring sitting on nothing but carpet. It wasn't dirty or nothing. She actually had her lil room kinda fixed up. She had her clothes and shoes color coordinated and neat, and she had posters of K.C. and Jo-Jo all over the walls. She

RESPECT REVENGE Pt. 1
"When Naptown Couldn't Sleep"

came back with some hair grease and some combs and told me to sit down on the floor, between her legs, while she sat in a chair. She had on some dark blue, blue jean shorts that was showing all of them pretty red thighs. She was wearing a white halter top and some low cut Reebok Classics, and some footies with little white ball on the back. Baby had some sexy ass legs on her too. Plus, that halter top was showing her stomach and really had a niggas' attention. When I sat down between her legs, my dick got harder than ten dollars' worth of jaw breakers. She was talking to me about her moving over here six months ago, and how everybody in the hood been trying to get at her. But I hardly heard anything she said because I was in my own little world, trying to figure out how I was going to get in them panties. I tried my hand to see how she would react. I ran my hand all the way up her leg, to the inner thigh and she didn't say nothing, so I tried again. This time she said,

"Boy you better stop, before you start some¬thing you can't finish."

I knew right then that it was on.

As soon as she finished my six braids straight to the back, I was on her. I stood up and took my shirt off, pretending to shake out the loose hairs, but was really showing her what I was working with. I could tell by the look on her face, she was impressed with a niggas' body. So I jumped straight to it.

"So what's up, you got a boyfriend or what?"
"Naw, I ain't got no man, if I did I wouldn't have you all up in my room."
"Well if you ain't got no man, then you wouldn't be wrong for fuckin' wit me then huh?"
"Fuckin' wit you how?"
"Now you wanna play all innocent huh? It looks like you done started something that you can't finish."

RESPECT REVENGE Pt. 1
"When Naptown Couldn't Sleep"

She knew I had her right there and she couldn't say nothing. So I pulled her in and just started kissing her on the neck.
"Ooh boy, that's my spot."
When I heard that, I turned it up a lil bit and started licking and sucking on her neck, slowly working my way to her mouth. I wasn't no pro at the four play game, so I just went for the kill after that.
 "Take them shorts off girl."
 "You take em' off for me."
I reached for her button and started wrestling trying to peel them little ass shorts off her ass. When I finally got em' off her panties were inside of them, so she was standing there in a halter top and some low top reeboks. I pulled her down onto her bed and lifted her shirt over her head and started suckin' on them pretty little titties, with the nice brown nipples. I took my middle finger and rubbed it up and down that lil hairy pussy, then slowly pushed it inside.
 "Ooh Shhh! That feel good Eric, don't stop."
She was feelin' that. Then she asked me,
 "Do you got a rubber?"
 "Naw I ain't got no rubber. You want me to stop?"
 "No, don't stop, but you better not nutt in me."
When she said that, I stood up and pulled my shorts and draws off and laid down on top of her. She reached down and grabbed my joint and rubbed it on the outside of her coochie, then put it in for me. She put her arms around my neck and looked me in the eye,
 "Please don't get me pregnant, pull it out before you cum okay."
 I said," I will, don't worry bout it."
"Please don't get me pregnant, pull it out before you cum okay."
 I said," I will, don't worry bout it."

RESPECT REVENGE Pt. 1
"When Naptown Couldn't Sleep"

Then I started pumpin' real slow. Shorty was wet like the fuckin ocean. Plus, her demonstration was tight and fitting a nigga like a glove. I picked up my pace and lifted them legs up and started trying to beat something; we was definitely makin' that clapping sound. She had her eyes closed and was biting on her top lip like she was trying to eat that mufucka. I knew I was doin' my thang a lil bit. Then just when I thought I was getting into the pussy kind of tough, I felt these nutts start to tingle and I knew what time it was. About 15 or 20 pumps later, I was telling myself that it was time to pull out, but my body wouldn't listen to me. Instead, I squeezed my ass cheeks together and let go of 15 months' worth of backed up babies as deep inside of her as I could.

She said, "I know you didn't just nutt in me did you?!"
"Naw I ain't nutt in you!"
"Yes you did, I can feel it. I better not get pregnant Eric!"
"You won't get pregnant; I can't have no kids."
"Boy shut up and get off of me and come on."

I got up and followed her to the bathroom. She got a rag out the closet and ran warm water on it and gently started cleaning off my dick. She looked up at me and said,

"So what was that? A hit it and quit it or what?"

I said, "It can be whatever you want it to be, I'm a leave it up to you. Just know that if I'm messing with you, I don't want you fuckin' wit nobody else."

"I ain't gonna mess with nobody but you, and if it was up to me you would be my man."

I said, "Then that's what it is then. After I said that she looked up and kissed me on the lips. I was feelin' baby girl.

I used Sheens phone to page Money. Now that I had got these nutts out of the sand, it was time to be about my paper. Money called back a few minutes later.

"Somebody hit a pager?"

RESPECT REVENGE Pt. 1
"When Naptown Couldn't Sleep"

I said, "Yeah, it's me Lil E."

"What's up lil homie, where you at?"

"I'm around on 26th street, next door to Lil Smurf's house."

"A'ight, I'm a swing through there in bout 15 minutes and scoop you up."

I said, "A'ight, I'm a be right here."

RESPECT REVENGE Pt. 1
"When Naptown Couldn't Sleep"

CHAPTER
10

I was sitting on Sheen's porch talkin' to my new boo, when I heard somebody coming down 26th Street beatin' that U.G.K. pocket full of stones out of their trunk. I saw this cocaine white, 4 door, 1985, Delta 88, sitting on 15' inch bars and vogues. This nigga's shit was clean and you could tell Money was feelin' it. His swagger was on one million, as he pulled up beating up the block. I told Sheen I would see her later and walked up on the car,
    "Jump in lil nigga, let's ride!"
I Jumped in and he pulled out the ash tray,
    "Fire that up, that's a blunt of that Charles Manson right there,"
I liked the nigga' Money already. Plus, I could tell he was about his business, because he had a gun metal grey .40 cal on his lap while we rode. We rode around and stopped here and there, while he dropped off dope and picked up money. After about four or five stops he pulled up in front of a duplex on Burdsal Parkway, a quiet block in our hood.
    He said, "Grab them Crown Royal bags out of the glove box for me."

RESPECT REVENGE Pt. 1
"When Naptown Couldn't Sleep"

We got out of the car and headed up to his crib. "Beep Beep!" He set his alarm, and we went in.

When we walked in the house, you could tell this was a bachelor's pad, cause there was blunt filling all over the coffee table, beer cans all over the place and about a hundred V.C.R. tapes up against the wall. Most of them porno's. He told me, "Have a seat, I'll be right down."

He snatched up his Crown Royal bags full of money and went upstairs.

While Money was upstairs doing whatever he was doing, I sat there on the couch thinking about all I had seen and heard over the last 24 hours. I see that Lil Smurf was just in the way out here. As long as he had weed to smoke, he was cool. The nigga Lil Dave was gone for a minute, only to be replaced by Money. Big June was still runnin' shit in the hood, and pretty much told me that, as long as I stayed loyal and was about my business, we was going to eat in these streets. I still hadn't went to check on this so called crack house my old man was supposed to be running.

"Damn lil nigga, you down here deep in thought ain't you?"

I didn't see or hear Money come back into the room.

I said, "Huh? Oh yeah, I was just trying to figure a few things out that's all."

He said, "Yeah, well here, this should help out a lil bit."

Money dropped two fat sacks of powder cocaine on my lap. He looked at me and said,

"Welcome home lil nigga. I know you official because for one, you are still breathing. I thought Big June was gettin' ready to rock you to sleep last night in that alley. Then for two, he gave you his stamp of approval, and he don't be just handing out hood passes to anybody. If you cool wit the O.G., then you definitely good with me."

I said, "Good lookin' out Money, I appreciate that."

RESPECT REVENGE Pt. 1
"When Naptown Couldn't Sleep"

Then he explained what was up in the hood from his own perspective.

"These lil niggas' round here don't want no money, so there is plenty of it for you to get. See this is how it go, Big June come up with four or five bricks, but the Big Homie ain't sellin' no dope. He straight puttin' down his robbery game. So he bring the dope to me and I serve it to the hood. These niggas' getting 9 ounces or 4 ½ and adding all that soda to they work and the fiends don't like it, so they take a long time to flip they shit, sometimes a week or a week and a half. So if you cook yo shit up raw with just enough bakin' soda to get it hard, then the fiends gonna love you and you gonna kill em' round here. Once you get your clientele up, you can flip a few ounces a day on that corner, that bitch be bumpin' like that."

So I asked Money, "How much I owe you for this?" He said, "You fresh home, so one of the ounces is on me, the other one you owe $800. for. That should be a start in the right direction."

I smiled from ear to ear at the love the nigga had just thrown my way. When I had left the streets, the most I had ever had was one ounce. And I had given Lil Smurf a quarter of that. I ain't been back in the hood 24 hours and already had two zips to my name. Now all I had to do was get it cooked up and dimed out and I was back in business.

I went to my old man Doc up on the corner and bought a box of baking soda and some sandwich bags and headed around to Smurf's crib. When I was walking up his steps, Trasheen popped her head out of her door and said,

"Where you goin'?"

I answered, "I'm bout to slide in here and handle some business."

"Handle what business?"

"Damn, who you working for, The police or the Feds?"

RESPECT REVENGE Pt. 1
"When Naptown Couldn't Sleep"

She got mad at that a lil bit. "Boy Boo, I ain't workin' for nobody."

It was 1:00 and I remember her saying that her mother didn't get home until 4 or 5:00, so I asked her,

"What time do your moms' walk through the door?"

"She a be here around 4 or 4:30 why?"

"Because I might can handle my business in your house if it's cool."

She said, "What you tryin' to do?"

"Let's just go in and I'll show you."

We went in and I headed straight to the kitchen and found just what I needed. A glass Pyrex measuring cup and a microwave. I pulled out the dope and her eyes lit up.

"Damn Eric, how much is that?"

"There you go again with all them questions."

"Boy shut up, I just asked because my lil brother be trying to hustle and that make his lil shit look small."

I handed her a sack of weed and two blunts and told her to give me some room and to let me work. When she saw that light green peeking at her through that bag, she grabbed it and hurried up and disappeared to the back porch. I got right down to business.

I smashed all the chunks of powder down to fine dust. Then put it in the Pyrex and added my soda. I added 7 grams of soda to the one ounce of coke and filled the jar half way up with water. I stuck it in the microwave for 5 minutes. After about 3 ½ minutes you could start to see the powder turning into thick, gummy, cocaine base. Then it was time for the magic trick. I took it out of the microwave and dropped three ice cubes in the jar and wallah! All the dope came together like butt cheeks. I poured off all the water and put the boulder onto a plate to dry. I did the same process with the other ounce and called Sheen in to help

RESPECT REVENGE Pt. 1
"When Naptown Couldn't Sleep"

me clean up the mess. Once the kitchen was spotless, we headed up to her room. I gave her $50 dollars to help me bag the shit up. I used a safety pin to break the rocks down into dime sized stones. As I broke em' down and sectioned em' off, she put em' into baggies. Then I would tie the knots and she would cut off the excess plastic with a razor blade. I bagged up 220 dimes out of one ounce and 212 out of the other one. That's like $2,000 per ounce, and that's good money. Just as we were gathering up all of the garbage, we heard the front door slam.
    "Sheen! Where you at girl?"
Her momma was hollering from way downstairs.
    "Oh shit my momma!"
Time had flown by while we was bagging up the work.
    Sheen said, "Clean this up while I go hold her off!"
She ran down the steps. When she left, I tried to figure out where I was going to stash my work at. I had considered Lil Smurf's at first, but now I had a better idea. I lifted up Sheen's bed and tucked it into the wood of the box spring. I had counted me out 100 dime pieces, and put em' in my draws. Sheen came runnin' up the steps just as I finished stashing the pack.
    "Come on we gotta get you outta here while she in the bathroom!"
Once we made it out of the house and onto the porch, we were cool. I told her where I had hid the work at and asked her if it was a'ight.
    "Yeah I guess, just make sure you look out for me and I'll hold you down."
Right then, I knew baby girl would be down for a nigga and would play a major part in me comin' up in them streets. You always needed someone on your team that you could trust and I had found me one. She said she had to go, pecked me on the lips, then took off in the house.

RESPECT REVENGE Pt. 1
"When Naptown Couldn't Sleep"

I took off down the street, looking for a ride to the nearest pager shop because I was back in the game. I had been thinkin' about this shit for the last fifteen months and now it was time to turn my thoughts into action…

RESPECT REVENGE Pt. 1
"When Naptown Couldn't Sleep"

CHAPTER 11

I ran through them two ounces in about five days on the corner, plus I had about six steady customers on my pager. I paid Money the $800 that I owed him, plus gave him $1,400 for two and a split. I had made 3,900 total because of the free pieces I had to give out in order to establish some clientele. So I had 2 and a quarter ounce, plus $1,700 in my pocket. Trasheen was my partner in this shit so I gave her $200 to go get her a few things from the mall. I figured if I flipped my money one or two more times, then I could buy me a lil hooptie to get around in. I took my granny a thousand dollars to hold

for me, she had no problem with it, she just told me to be careful. I was definitely being that, I had bought a .357 snub nose from a smoker and kept it on me at all times because that corner was hectic and you had to be ready for anything. I kept the same routine for the next few months and ended up with $7,500 in my stash and was running through 4 ½ ounces every week. I had been with Money every day and happened to be with him one day when I got a 911 page from Trasheen.

    I said, "Hey Money, let me use your phone real

RESPECT REVENGE Pt. 1
"When Naptown Couldn't Sleep"

quick." Money spoke into his phone, "Juan-C, let me hit you back in a few, my lil nigga want to use this phone. Man you better swing past pops crib, he been askin' bout you, and you ain't got no excuse cause he right there in your neck of the woods. I'm a catch you later cuz."
Then he hung up and gave me the phone. I called Sheen's number back and it was her mother. She told me I needed to come around there real quick.
"Hey Money, swing me around to my girl's crib right fast." He could tell by the look on my face that something was up.
So he asked, "Is everything all good my nigga?"
"I don't know, but I'll see in a minute."
We pulled up and I hopped out and ran up on the porch. Ms. Aggie saw me comin' and said,
"Come on in here boy."
Ms. Aggie was Sheen's mother. She was cool, she knew about me and baby sexing and everything, she just told us to use protection so we didn't make her a grandmother at 36.
"You done exactly what I asked you not to do huh?"
"Naw Ms. Aggie, what you talkin' bout?"
"That girl done missed her period, plus she been throwing up for the last two days."
When she said that my heart dropped.
I said, "We been usin' rubbers."
"Boy shut yo mouth! Ya'll been up in that room humpin' like rabbits and you ain't putting nothin' on that lil thang every time. I was young before too remember."
I asked, "Where she at right now?"
"She up in her room lookin' silly, gone up there and talk to her."
I hollered out and told Money that I was cool and I would get up wit him later and he rolled out. I went up to Sheen's room and she was laid across the bed crying.

RESPECT REVENGE Pt. 1
"When Naptown Couldn't Sleep"

I said, "What's up baby girl, you a'ight?"
    "Naw I ain't a'ight! What am I gonna do?"
I answered her, "What you mean? We a be straight, I'm a keep grindin' and we will get us a place and shit a be straight."
    "You serious Eric?"
"Yeah I'm serious, it ain't the end of the world."
When I said that she got up and hugged me around the neck with tears running down her face.
"I love you Eric."
 I'd never told her before, but now seemed like a good time to come clean.
"I love you too baby girl." Then I laid there with her until she fell asleep.
The next day I slid over Big June's crib to chill and smoke something with the big homie. I tapped on the door.
    "What's up Lil E?"
    "What's up Big Homie?"
He said, "I ain't doin shit, just layin back gettin my thoughts together so I can keep the hood afloat. I been hearing bout you up on that corner. They say you out there doin' you baby boy."
"Yeah, I been making it happen, plus Money be blessin' a nigga, so he make it easy for me to get ahead out here."
June said, "I told you Money all good, plus he said you was a go getta'."
It felt good gettin' praise from both of my O.G.'s, because they was the ones who could make it happen for you in a major way out here. Then Big June got real serious on me.
    "Listen to this and tell me if you think you ready. I got this lick comin' up where one of my lil bitch's done peeped game on one of these pillow talkin' ass niggas'. She say the nigga be coppin' his work from these Mexicans next door to her. He be using her apartment to make his move. She calls him when the

RESPECT REVENGE Pt. 1
"When Naptown Couldn't Sleep"

Mexicans give her the okay. She don't know exactly what he be gettin', but he go in with a book bag and come out with a duffle bag. So we talking bout some serious weight here. I had my squad already lined up, but one of my lil soldiers got locked up and he ain't got no bond, so I have to replace him. I'm a probably have you hold down the door and play look out while we in there. Can you handle that?"

I didn't want to act as if I had been there before and jump out there like, "Hell yeah!" and blow my chances to fuck wit some heavy weights. But I wasn't gonna pass up on this chance either. I had heard about some of Big June's demonstrations. He was serious, plus he play for keeps. So I answered the only way I felt I could,
"You know I'm down for whatever. But you gotta school me so I don't fuck up."

"See, that's why I fuck wit you lil nigga, you use your head for more than just a hat rack. Keep peepin' game and be a student, and you will make it out here, cause half these niggas can't think past go. If you can out think a nigga, you can win every time."

For the next week, whenever I wasn't on the block gettin' money, I was over Big June crib. Me, him, and Cookie face. Cookie face was a couple years older than me, and he was known to be a straight killer. He didn't do no rappin' at all. He just did as he was told, and loved puttin' his murder game down. Cookie was about 6"3 and 220 pounds of solid muscle. He was jet black with a short nappy fro that seemed like he never got cut, but still stayed the same size. He use to have real bad skin, but he had grown out of it, but the name cookie face just stuck with him. He use to be Lil Dave's muscle up on the corner, but once Lil Dave went off to the joint, Cookie fell under Big June for guidance. We went over the plan so many times, that we all knew it like the back of our

RESPECT REVENGE Pt. 1
"When Naptown Couldn't Sleep"

hands. The big day had finally arrived and I went over to Sheens crib where I had been staying. Ms. Aggie had been letting me stay in the crib as long as I paid the utilities and put a lil food in the fridge. I crept in the back door and into bed with baby girl, and laid there in deep thought well into the night, thinking about how tomorrow would either make me or break me ...

RESPECT REVENGE Pt. 1
"When Naptown Couldn't Sleep"

CHAPTER 12

We all met up over Big June's crib at 1:00 in the afternoon. We locked and loaded our straps. We made sure to load up everything with gloves on, so we didn't leave prints on shell casings. I had my .357 snub on me. Plus, June gave me a .9 mm Gloc that held 16 in the clip and one in the hole. Big June had a .40 cal and he loaded up a AK.47 with a 30 round clip. Cookie had a .44 bulldog, a .45 automatic, plus a knife that would have made Rambo jealous. Big June threw me a pillow case with a brand new roll of duct tape, a butane lighter, two tennis balls, a hammer and a box of nails. I didn't understand some of the items, but I was responsible for carrying the pillow case, so I assumed I'd soon see what the extra items were for.

    We all dressed in the same shit. Big June was specific in what we were to wear. All black, with hoodies and runnin' shoes. He gave us some brown gloves and bandana's and asked us was we ready to go. The looks and the mood in the room said it all. Niggas' definitely had on their game faces.

    We all hopped in an all black "85 box Chevy, with tinted windows and rolled out with Cookie behind the wheel.

RESPECT REVENGE Pt. 1
"When Naptown Couldn't Sleep"

We pulled up into some apartments on the north side of town and parked between a big brown van and a truck and waited for Big June to place his phone call. He pulled his burn-out phone out of the glove box and started dialing numbers. You could hear the girl when she answered.
"Hello?"
"What's up baby girl, this the Big Fella."
"What's up Big June? Where you at?"
"I'm where I'm supposed to be at, look out the window."
Just then the blinds in the apartment directly across from us started moving.
She said," I see you."
"Well what time is he supposed to come through?"
"I'm supposed to call him when the Mexican guy next door bang on my wall. After that, he will be pulling up in exactly 20 minutes."
Big June said, "A'ight, dial my number and hang up right after you place your call to him okay?"
I guess she said okay, because after that he said,
"Okay baby girl," then hung up.
The plan was this, when she made the call, I would hop in the brown van parked next to us, then pull around to the front of the apartments. Once I saw the nigga in his money green, Nissan Maxima with the five star rims, I was to pull in behind him. When he pulled into this section of the apartments, I would bump his bumper kind of hard, causing him to either get out and inspect the dam¬age, or run up on the van trippin'. Then Big June would come from his blind side and force him into the van, while Cookie ran up on his partner in his passenger seat and lay iron on him, forcing him out the car and into the van too. Once we got both of them in the van, I would hop out and move the Maxima while Big June got behind the wheel of the van. All that

RESPECT REVENGE Pt. 1
"When Naptown Couldn't Sleep"

went exactly as planned and we ended up back in the van. Big June took all the money out of the book bag and replaced it with the bundled up newspaper that he had stashed in the van earlier. Then he laid the plan out to the nigga. "Look this is what's gonna happen. We gonna leave yo buddy here in the van. Me and you are gonna go in here and make the deal with these fuckin' wetbacks. If you move wrong or even act like you gonna tip em' off, then you getting' it on the spot and your buddy will die slow. Do you understand?" The nigga could tell he was in a no win situation, so he nodded slow with a look of defeat on his face. Part two of the lick was to get inside of the Mexicans crib and lay them down too. The nigga we had, whose name was C-note, grabbed the bag that June had stuffed with the dummy money and him and Big June got out and headed towards the crib.

 I was supposed to stay in the van until I saw the curtains move in the crib. Cookie had already slid off in ol' girls spot with the AK. Once June and C-Note got inside of the Mexicans spot, I was to push send on the cell phone. That would ring ol' girls phone, letting Cookie know to go out of her back door and kick in the back door of the Mexicans and take control of the situation with the chopper. Once again, everything went as planned and we was one step closer. The dude that was in the back of the van was duct taped from head to toe like a fuckin' mummy, so he wasn't goin' nowhere. Once the curtains moved, I grabbed the pillowcase and went to the front door and just walked in.

 The two Mexicans were laid out on the floor spread eagle, with Cookie standing over them with the chopper trained and ready to go. They were both speaking rapid Spanish, until Big June barked,

 "Shut them mufuckas up!"

 Cookie came down with the butt of the chopper on the

RESPECT REVENGE Pt. 1
"When Naptown Couldn't Sleep"

back of one of their heads, knocking him out cold and putting a nice sized gash across his shit. Big June looked at me and said,
"Hold the heat on this nigga C-note while I tie these Mexican mufuckas' up!"
He walked over and stomped on the head of the Mexican who was still conscious with so much force, that I thought he had killed him. Then he stripped them both butt naked and taped them to separate chairs. He then knocked C-note out cold with a big right hand and told me to tape him up. Once we had the whole situation under control and everybody bound and subdued, he told me to go hold down the front door, while him and Cookie got down to the business.

He slapped the face of the Mexican who was in charge until he regained consciousness.
Then asked him, "Where them birds at poppi?"
The Mexican answered, "No comprend'e, Me don't speak no English!"
He said that with a smirk on his face like he was the smartest mufucka' in the room. Big June looked at him and said,
"I thought you might say that, but I'm a real good English teacher, I'll have you speakin' English in no time."
Then he looked at Cookie and gave him the nod. Cookie's face lit up like he had been waiting on this part all day long. He went into the pillow case and got one of the tennis balls and stuffed it into the Mexican's mouth, then wrapped duct tape around his head. Now amigo didn't look so smart. His eyes were darting around the room like it was a thousand people in there. Cookie then pulled out the butane lighter and lifted my mans' nutt sack up with a gloved hand and held the flame to his scrotum. The Mexican tried his best to holler out in pain, but with a tennis ball taped in his mouth, all he could do was grunt and moan. Tears came rollin' down his face immediately and the room

RESPECT REVENGE Pt. 1
"When Naptown Couldn't Sleep"

started to smell like burnt flesh and hair. After about ten seconds of constant flame to the sack, his shit was visibly blistered and swollen to almost twice the normal size. Big June stepped in and with a fake Spanish accent he asked,

"Do poppy speak English now?"

The Mexican just stared at him with death in his eyes. If looks could kill, Big June would have dropped dead on the spot.

June said, "Oh, so you still don't want to talk huh?" Then looked at Cookie and once again gave him a nod. Cookie went back into the pillow case and pulled out a big ass nail. I started to wonder, what the fuck he gonna do with that? He held the '7-inch nail under the flame of the butane lighter until the whole damn nail glowed red from the heat. Then he grabbed poppy's dick and shoved the nail down in his pee hole in one swift motion. I closed my eyes because it hurt me to just see it. I was supposed to be watching out of this window for any surprise visitors, but this shit here had my undivided attention. I thought he would let out another gut wrenching scream, or at least try to, but instead, he just passed out from the pain.

"I bet that mufucka' speak English when he wake up," said Big June.

Cookie pulled out a hammer and stood over my man, waiting for him to wake up. The whole time all this was going on, the other Mexican is over there ballin' his eyes out and mumbling. It looked as if he was praying. Poppy started to stir and when he came to, he looked at his mutilated dick and started crying instantly. See the nail was now stuck because it had melted his flesh like plastic and now the nail and his skin were like one. Cookie grabbed his dick with the hammer in hand and put the part of the hammer that you remove nails with, around the end of the nail as if he was getting' ready to pull it out of a regular piece of wood. Poppy's head went up and down so fast as if to say he was ready

RESPECT REVENGE Pt. 1
"When Naptown Couldn't Sleep"

to cooperate. Big June said,
"Oh, you speak English now huh?"
Poppy's head just kept going up and down. Cookie ripped the tape off of his mouth and pulled out the tennis ball,
"Upstairs! In the bathroom, under the sink! The wall under there is fake, push on it and you will find what you are looking for!"
Big June smiled and said, "I knew you could do it Poppy, all it took was a little time!"
Then he took off up the stairs like he weighed 150lbs. Once he got up there we heard him yell out,
"Bingo!"
Then he came runnin' down the steps with a black duffle bag with six kilos of cocaine in it.
"Nice doin bidness with you Poppy! I'm sure this ain't the whole load, but it will definitely do."
He threw me the bag and said,
"Hold on to that while I go next door and break ol' girl off."
He slipped out the back of the apartment we were in and into the crib of his broad. He was over there for maybe two minutes when we heard a single gunshot. **"Boc!"**
He came back into the apartment we were in and said,
"She been paid in full. Clean up in here Cookie and we will be waiting in the van."
As we were heading out of the door, I saw Cookie pull out that giant Rambo knife and start hacking away at the throat of the nigga' C-note. I never heard a gunshot so I assumed he killed all three of them the same way. When he came out he jumped in the Chevy we had come in and followed us in the van. When we left there it was 8:00p.m. and dark outside. I was wondering what we was going to do with ol' boy in the back of the van. Then we pulled over on this dark side street and Big June killed the lights. He got out and grabbed dude out of the back and slung him

RESPECT REVENGE Pt. 1
"When Naptown Couldn't Sleep"

over his shoulder and carried him to the back of this abandoned house. He threw the nigga on the ground, then said to me, "Take all that tape off his ass."
I started pullin' the duct tape off the nigga and when I finished Big June looked me in the eye and said,
      "Now put his ass to sleep."
I couldn't believe what I had just heard. I had shot one nigga. Even shot at a few more. But never had I up close and personal taken a man's life. I pulled out my .357 and stood over dude, staring into his pleading eyes. So much shit flashed through my mind in a matter of seconds. Then I pulled the trigger twice, and watched what a close range shot from a- .357, did to a human face. I stood over him for another 10 seconds and as I watched the blood leave his body, I felt the innocents leave out of mine. I knew there would be no turning back now. I was in the streets ten toes deep. This was my world now, so I would have to accept everything that came with it.

RESPECT REVENGE Pt. 1
"When Naptown Couldn't Sleep"

CHAPTER 13

Trasheen had the baby in the summer of "95". It was a boy and we named him Eric Jr. I had come up heavy after the Big June lick. It turned out that the nigga C-note had $70,000 dollars in that book bag, plus we had got the six bricks from Poppy and them. My share was one of the bricks and $20,000 dollars. It wasn't exactly an even split, but I definitely wasn't complaining.

    Me and Sheen had a nice two-bedroom town house on the far Westside of town out by the airport. I was pushing a 1993 Lexus coupe, and baby had a cream colored 1992 Camry. Plus, I had a 1976 Malibu, all black, sittin' on factory rims with tinted windows that I hustled out of. I was coppin two or three bricks at a
time from Big June and was pushin' weight in the hood to the youngsters. You could get anything from a quarter ounce, to a four and a split from me any day of the week. I even had Lil Smurf hustlin' good, instead of just being in the way. I had went and pulled my two niggas off the block and had them with me all the time. They wasn't really hustlers, but they was bout that gun play. Plus, they put me on with them

RESPECT REVENGE Pt. 1
"When Naptown Couldn't Sleep"

when we use to play the block on the late nighters. These two niggas were the last of the real Bottom Boys. P.U. was the bigger of the two. Fam was 6 foot one and 190 lbs. with a strong slender frame. He had some nappy ass dreads and a full beard. He had these little beady eyes that if you looked into them, would let you know to find someone else to play with. All he ever wore were different types of army fatigues and Timberland boots. The name P.U. stood for pretty ugly. Because fuckin' wit him, that's how shit could get real quick. The other nigga name was Lil Lucky. Lil Lucky was 5 foot 5 inches tall and was high yellow with long corn rows. His appearance would cause the average nigga to underestimate him because he was a pretty boy and a small one at that. But the people who knew, knew he was one of the most dangerous mufuckas' you never wanted to fuck with. The ones that didn't know, by the time he found out, it was most likely too late. The lil nigga had a vicious little man complex and he was a fool with that pistol. Drama was what the lil dude lived for. And that was my squad, Me, Smurf, Lil Lucky, and P.U.

  Shit was all good for "96" and "97". We was eating and shinning and my clique had the hood on smash. We had whips, we had hoes, and we had respect. The only competition we had was the nigga Money and his new crew of hustlers. See after we hit the lick with the nigga Big June, Money felt a certain kind of way about me and Cookie gettin' blessed like we did. Then the fact that we wasn't going through him to get our work, but directly to Big June, it put a dent in his pocket cause he wasn't the only one in the hood serving weight. He had these lames in the hood that he put on running around with their chest poked out, mean muggin' and murda mouthing niggas';

RESPECT REVENGE Pt. 1
"When Naptown Couldn't Sleep"

Knowing that they guns don't bust like that. But sometimes, having a lil paper make a lame forget that he really a lame. You can buy a lot of things when your money get right, but heart ain't one of em'. Money and his peons were starting to get beside themselves in the hood, and they was about to show just how much ...

RESPECT REVENGE Pt. 1
"When Naptown Couldn't Sleep"

CHAPTER 14

Big June called my cell phone while I was over my grannies one afternoon.

"What's up Big Homie?" I answered.

"Ain't nothin', I need to see you bout some business as soon as possible."

I said, "A'ight, I'm a swing through your spot as soon as I leave my grandmother crib, is that cool?"

"Yeah, that a work, plus that will give me time to get the niggas' Money and Rico out of here."

Rico was Money's new right hand man. Rico was a cool nigga, but he was the type that couldn't think for himself. If Money say it, then Rico took it as law. Them type of niggas' can't be trusted cause if the nigga that got his hand up the back of the niggas' shirt makin' him talk fall out with you, then you got to start watching the dummy as well, because he don't have a mind of his own.

    I finished my regular Sunday conversation that I usually had with Granny, and told her that I loved her. Before I left, I slid in on Keisha and hit her off with a couple hundred and asked her about some nigga in her neighborhood that

RESPECT REVENGE Pt. 1
"When Naptown Couldn't Sleep"

Auntie said she been spending too much time with. I knew if she was messing with one of them Brightwood niggas', then he was probably a dope boy. That's why I always put a lil money in her pockets, so she wouldn't have to ask a nigga in the street for nothing. But lil cuz had grown up to be a dime and you couldn't keep her away from dudes if you tried. I kissed her on the cheek and told her to watch herself out there, and I rolled out.
    It was 7:35 p.m., I'll never forget it. My cell phone rang and I picked it up on the first ring.
"Yeah, who dis'."
At first, all I heard was what sounded like a scuffle, then I heard a familiar voice say,
"Nigga, you know what it is! Where the rest of this shit at?!"
I was confused at first, then I heard,
    "I ain't tellin' you shit nigga, you gonna kill me anyway, cause you know if you don't, then I'm a wipe out your whole fuckin' bloodline!"
 It was the voice of Big June. My heart was beating a mile a minute and I hit the gas trying to get across town and come to the Big Homies rescue. I kept the phone to my ear as I dashed through traffic trying to make every light. Then I heard the unthinkable. **"Boc! Boc! Boc!"** Then I heard a loud thump like someone hit the floor. I started yelling into the phone, "Hello! Hello!"
Then that familiar voice that I heard asking Big June where it was at earlier, picked up the phone.
"Hello? Hello?" And then I instantly recognized the voice. It was Money ....
They had just killed Big June ...

RESPECT REVENGE Pt. 1
"When Naptown Couldn't Sleep"

CHAPTER 15

I hung up my phone and a single tear streamed down my face. I knew what had to be done, and I knew who had to do it. Big June had taught me everything I know about these streets. He had been grooming me since the very first day he met me. He was definitely my O.G. and I couldn't 't let him go out unavenged by the hands of a jealous hearted snake, that he had blessed just as much as he had blessed me. I got on my phone and called P.U. and Lucky and told them to meet me in front of Big June's house immediately.

    When I pulled up, they were already there and the police had the spot yellow taped off. It was about fifty mufuckas' out there, people crying and mourning the loss of the neighborhood O.G. I got out slowly and P.U. asked me, how did I know what was up?

    I said, "I will fill you in later my nigga."
After they hauled away the body, I hopped in the Lexus and jumped on the freeway. I had no destination, but a blunt and the freeway always put a nigga at ease. I figured I had the upper hand because I knew Money and Rico were the last ones to see Big June alive. Money had made the mistake

RESPECT REVENGE Pt. 1
"When Naptown Couldn't Sleep"

of picking up the phone that Big June had hit the send button on. When he did that, it automatically redialed the last number called, which was me. See, the Big Homie wasn't stupid, he knew death was inevitable, so he made sure that a real nigga knew what went down, so this fake, back stabbing nigga Money wouldn't get away like that. So my plan was to wait until after the funeral, then make Money's life shorter by a whole lot of years. While I was thinking this, a thought crossed my mind, If Big June didn't give them niggas' the rest of the dope, then it was most likely still in the stash spot. Under the dog house in his backyard ...

    The funeral was six days later at a funeral home right outside the hood and it was just as ghetto fabulous as I had expected. There were ballers from all over the city, many of em' I knew, a few of em' I didn't. Most of them were there to show the Big Fella some love, but just as many were there to make sure the nigga was really dead. Me, Lil Smurf, P.U., and Lil Lucky walked in and posted up around the O.G. 's casket for a full two minutes, just taking in the sight of the realest nigga we knew stretched out in front of us with all this fucking make up on his forehead trying to cover up the wound he suffered when he died. Then all at the same time, we turned and faced the crowd and looked damn near everybody in attendance in the eye. I had already told fam' and them the play with the nigga's Money and Rico, but I told them not to tip their hands until the time was right. We was just making sure niggas was uncomfortable, but still not revealing that we knew who was involved. When my eyes crossed Money's, he held my gaze for a few seconds then looked away. But I could have swore he had a smirk on his face. Little did he know, I would have the last laugh when it was all said and done.

    After the funeral was over and Big June was lowered into the ground. This nigga from the Eastside named Jake eased up beside me as I stood over the six-foot hole looking down

RESPECT REVENGE Pt. 1
"When Naptown Couldn't Sleep"

on my nigga. "What's up Lil E? How you holding up?"
I said, "I'm good fam, just trippin' over the loss of my nigga."
"Yeah, I can feel that. You know me and Big June was real close and we did a lot of business over the last couple of years and he spoke real highly of you. I know he would have wanted me to move forward and keep this shit rollin with you in his place, so I'm a give you my number and when you ready, we can make it snow out here for real. I got a hell of a plug and I'm a give em' to you for the same price I was giving them to Big June for."
I turned and looked Jake in the face and asked him,
"Why would you do that for me?"
He looked me dead in the eye and said,
"Because whoever killed my little brother, I know you gonna make em' pay. "
When he said that, I looked at him hard for the first time and I'll be damned if him and the Big Homie didn't look just alike. I showed Jake some love and slid off with his number locked in my phone. Later that night, I put on all black and crept into Big June's backyard. The Pitbull he had was gone because the police had called the dog pound and had the dog removed because the owner was dead, so it was easy to get to his old house. As soon as I lifted it up, I knew that I had been right. There was eight tightly wrapped bricks of cocaine staring me right in the face.
But I promised myself that I wouldn't bust open not even one of em' until everybody that had a hand in the death of my nigga, was no longer walking the face of this Earth ....

RESPECT REVENGE Pt. 1
"When Naptown Couldn't Sleep"

CHAPTER
16

By the time the Big June situation came about, I had been having money for a while and with money come haters, and with haters come problems. So I had developed my own little arsenal of weapons, I had more guns than I could shoot. I also had a clique of wolves that couldn't wait to draw blood. I didn't realize how many niggas' I actually had at my disposal, because I had never been into letting my right hand know what my left hand was doing. I had sort of become insulated from a lot of nigga's because I had started serving nigga's weight and letting them feed their own soldiers. But if you are the soldier of a nigga who's a soldier to me, then ultimately you are a soldier in my own army. I gathered together the niggas from the Hard-Part who I knew were loyal to me and two who I knew were extremely loyal to Big June. We all met at Riverside Park for a late night basketball game under the park lights, so as to not spook anybody from the hood who just happen to see us. It was Me, P.U., Smurf, Lucky, Cookie, and this cat named Falcon Eddie. I even extended an invite to the nigga Money, knowing he wouldn't come. The nigga said, "I don't ball on no court, I ball in these streets, ya'll

RESPECT REVENGE Pt. 1
"When Naptown Couldn't Sleep"

nigga's go ahead." I figured the nigga wouldn't see it for what it was and refuse. But I was actually forming my team and getting them ready for war, and an official takeover of the whole hood. Everybody started pulling up and arriving right on time, with the exception of Lil Smurf. This nigga had no sense of responsibility unless it concerned him and I knew that, but he had four or five lil goons that would come in handy. The nigga Falcon Eddie was an old school cat from the hood, a straight jack boy. He came up in the era where everybody didn't sell dope. Some niggas would rob you, then flaunt yo shit right in front of you and dare you to trip. He was one of them. He had a few other old heads on his team that were about they issue, they all snorted that powder like it was going out of style, but it never decreased their reputation as cold killers. Falcon Eddie and Big June had hooked up on a few missions and Falcon definitely respected the Big Fella's Gangsta. But Falcon was only loyal to him and his crew, so I knew the only way to get him on board was to appeal to his greed. I just wanted him and his henchmen to start terrorizing Money's five block radius in the hood. They had 15 or 20 hustlers workin' them blocks 24/7. They had gone virtually un - touched because of the umbrella of Big June. But today, I was pulling that umbrella down and letting the storm come through. Once I told Falcon that he had the green light to do what he wanted on them blocks, him and his main man O.G. Vester rolled out. He had this smile on his face that said he had been itching to get at these nigga's pockets for a while. I knew Money had his weight, his soldiers, and his guns up, and he would be kind of hard to touch. I mean, if a nigga wanted to go commando and just start choppin' at his car in traffic, then yeah, it wouldn't be hard at all. But we already had homicide detectives crawling around the hood asking everybody questions cause bodies stayed dropping around the way. So I figured we would give Falcon and them a week or two, to expose

RESPECT REVENGE Pt. 1
"When Naptown Couldn't Sleep"

them cowards for what they really were. After a few of them dropped, then Money would figure they were beefin' wit Falcon and his clique of hard hitters. By then they would be weak and vulnerable and we would come through and clean it up. See, most of them lames would tuck tail and run at the first sign of blood, and that would leave the real ones to deal with the drama. They would be enough to deal with Falcon and them, but the element of surprise from us, would be too much to stand. Then I would crush Money for good, avenging the O.G., plus, at the same time take over them blocks and become the new nigga to see when it came to the Hard-Part ...

RESPECT REVENGE Pt. 1
"When Naptown Couldn't Sleep"

CHAPTER
17

Falcon and his men started eating them dudes alive. They was hittin' their corner boys left and right. They killed three of them on the first night out to show that it wasn't a game, and that they meant business. About a week after the first action, they fucked around and snatched up one of Money's main players and held him in an abandoned crib on one of my blocks, and made him tell them exactly how to get at Money and Rico. Money didn't show his face too often, but did most of his business through Rico. Rico on the other hand was very accessible, he had a lil spot on the other side of town, in the hood known as Brightwood, and Corey was one of the ones who could go out there and get some work from him.

So the nigga Corey, who was stuck in the abandoned house with the killers', told them he would set the nigga Rico up for them in order to free himself. So Falcon set up the move and him and his crew stood by while Corey made the phone call. Rico answered on the second ring.
"Yeah, what's up?"
"What's up Rico, this Corey."
Then Rico said, "What's up my nigga? Where you at?"

RESPECT REVENGE Pt. 1
"When Naptown Couldn't Sleep"

"I'm in the hood an I'm finished with that; I need to see you."
"Damn, you through already? You been on it out there huh?"
 "Yeah, a lot of these nigga's is layin low because of these robberies and shit, but I got to get me regardless."
 "I can feel that. Come on through to the spot out East, I got you fam'."
 Corey said, "A'ight", then hung up.
 Falcon said, "You did good, but this shit far from over. Now tell me the set up out there."
Corey answered and said, "Them niggas' is real laxed out there because they ain't never had no problems, but the dude on the door be strapped though."
Falcon said, "I'm a tell you straight up, if you lying to me, you will be the first one to get it. You feel me?"
"Yeah O.G., I'm just trying to make it. I ain't trying to die over these niggas' shit!"
Falcon smiled on the outside, but he wanted to kill the bitch nigga right then. He couldn't stand a rat mufucka who would turn on his own in order to save himself.

   One hour later, Falcon and his squad rolled out in two separate cars; it was seven people in all. Falcon, plus his five hitters and the nigga Corey. Falcon couldn't figure how they would get in the front door undetected, so he opted to have Corey knock on the door and once someone answered, just run in guns blazing. He sent two of his best up on the front porch with pump shotguns loaded down with deer slugs. Then two more would follow them with choppers to clean up anything they missed. Then him and his right hand man would pull up the rear and catch anything coming out the back door. When the first two were in place on the porch, Falcon sent Corey to the door.
"Knock-Knock-Knock!"
  "Who dat?"

RESPECT REVENGE Pt. 1
"When Naptown Couldn't Sleep"

"It's me Corey!" The fat mufucka who answered the door was supposed to be security, but as soon as he saw Corey was alone, he turned around and walked off into the house, with a .50 cal Desert Eagle down by his side. He started to say,
"Yeah, the nigga Rico been expec ..."
And before he could even finish, one of the shotguns roared, letting one of the deer slugs tear through his back and put his guts all over the pool table that was sittin' in the middle of the floor. As soon as Corey heard the blast he attempted to flee deeper into the house, causing the trigger man to open up and take his head clean off his shoulders. The first two gunman turned their attention to a hallway to the left of the door because they heard scrambling down that way, plus there were rooms on both sides. The AK's came runnin' through the door soon after and both ran straight to the steps. Falcon sensing that the first floor was secured,
      kicked in the back door and came in aiming for anything that moved. Rico was upstairs when he heard the two shotgun blast. He quickly pushed the female that he was laid up with off of him and reached and grabbed the twin Gloc's that he kept on the nightstand beside the bed. He grabbed her arm and pulled her into the hallway with him to use as a human shield. When he saw the nigga with the "AK-47" bend the corner coming off the stairs, he pulled the girl in front of him and unloaded one of his Gloc's into one of Falcon's soldiers, filling him with .9mm slugs and dropping him instantly. The other "AK" wielder, seeing his partner flat lined with blood coming out of his ears and mouth, immediately turned the whole hallway into something straight out of Iraq. Emptying his whole 30 round clip into nothing but air. Rico had dipped back into the room he had come out of. When he heard the break in shooting, he figured whoever it was, was trying to re-load, so he came out dumping slugs blindly. He knew

RESPECT REVENGE Pt. 1
"When Naptown Couldn't Sleep"

he had found his mark, because he heard someone moan and then drop like a ton of bricks. He then took baby girl, who was crying so hard that she could barely stand, to the top of the steps and pushed her down and watched as Falcon filled her up with .40 caliber rounds. Rico stood at the top of the steps for a brief second and locked eyes with Falcon. Falcon fired at him, hitting him in the stomach once and Rico took off into the nearest room to hide because he didn't have any more bullets in his gun. He slammed the door behind him, then quickly pulled out his cell phone and dialed Money's number.

"Come on, come on, Pick up!" "Hello?"
"Money, It's me man! They got me! Corey set me up! Falcon and his goon's are in my spot right now and I'm hit!"
Money said, "What !!"

"You heard me! They must be behind all our spots and workers gettin' hit out west!" As soon as he said that, the door came flying off the hinges, and a masked man with a pump shotgun came in pointing it right in his face.

"**Boom!** Clack -Clack **Boom!**" and all of Rico's last thoughts were splattered all over the wall behind him. Falcon and his two remaining goons gathered up all of the dope and money they had found in the rooms downstairs and made their exit to the distant sound of police sirens ...

RESPECT REVENGE Pt. 1
"When Naptown Couldn't Sleep"

CHAPTER 18

Late that same night, on the 11:00 news, the top story was a multiple killing on the Eastside of the city in the Brightwood area.

"Breaking news, six confirmed dead in what appears to be a drug related robbery. Police say at least 4 masked gunman invaded the home of this man, 24-year-old Rico Clemons. Found dead were also 22-year-old Corey Staten, and 27-year-old Courtney Collins, who was found with a major gunshot wound to the back. Two yet to be identified black males, who appear to be in their late thirties were also found in the house. Also, we have a 17-year-old Black Female identified as Keisha Hunt, who was found with multiple gunshot wounds to the body, she also died at the scene. Police say they had been watching the residence for weeks trying to piece together enough evidence to get a search warrant for the home. Police found lots of drug paraphernalia and a large scale they say was used for weighing large sums of narcotics. Also found were an array of automatic weapons. Police have no leads and ask anyone with information to contact crime stoppers at 272- tips, again, that's 272- tips. Back to you

RESPECT REVENGE Pt. 1
"When Naptown Couldn't Sleep"

Tom." This news bit had just said, "17-year-old Keisha Hunt." That was my little cousin. What was she doin in there? Who had killed her? I sat there in deep contemplation, thinking about what I had just heard, until my phone pulled me out of my trance.
  "Hello?"
"Baby, it's me granny." You could tell by her voice that she had been crying.
She said, "I know you have either heard or saw the news by now, but Keisha is dead."
 Hearing her say those words brought tears to my eyes and rage to my heart.
 She continued, "Now baby, I know you are upset, but don't go out there and do nothing stupid, promise me now?"
  "I promise I'll think before I act granny."
"Let God handle this, you hear me son?"
"I hear you granny. Where is Auntie Rhonda? How is she holding up?"
"She cried herself to sleep, she ain't in no shape to talk right now, but come and see her in the morning okay? "
 "I will granny and I love you okay?"
"I love you too baby and I'll see you soon."
As soon as she hung up, I called Falcon and told him to meet me at the same park we had met at the first time in an hour. I got P.U., Lucky, Cookie, and Lil Smurf and explained what was up, and told them that the drama starts now. I sent Cookie, Lil Smurf and Lil Lucky to strap up and clear out the five blocks that Money claimed as his own. I took P.U. with me to the park to meet with Falcon. He arrived not long after I did. I walked up on Falcon and said, "What's up O.G., what happened out there tonight?
  "Man youngin', shit got crazy. I lost some soldiers out there, but we came off with a couple of

RESPECT REVENGE Pt. 1
"When Naptown Couldn't Sleep"

bricks and $40,000. Then I asked him, "What happened with that girl?" (not revealing that she was family)
"Man I heard world war two going on upstairs and was getting ready to head up when she came flying down. I mean literally, and I was already on pins and needles, so I just started dumping. By the time I realized it was a female, I had shot her 8 times. I looked up to the top of the stairs and saw the bitch nigga Rico standing there. He had pushed her down at me like a human sacrifice."
Hearing him say the nigga Rico had sacrificed baby cuz infuriated me, but I kept my cool because even though she had died by the gun of the nigga Falcon, she had died from the actions of that bitch nigga Rico. Rico was dead and so I couldn't punish him, so I knew that my hate for the nigga Money had just been multiplied by a million. I told the cat Falcon that I would take over from there and he could gone ahead and enjoy the fruits of his labor. It was now time for me and mines to turn it up ...

RESPECT REVENGE Pt. 1
"When Naptown Couldn't Sleep"

CHAPTER
20

The next few days were very stressful for me and my family. My grandmother was very quiet for the most part, trying to be the rock that my auntie needed in order to make it through the ordeal of burying her only child. The process of going to the police station and answering questions, identifying the body, and preparing for the funeral has sucked the light and life out of auntie's once radiant eyes.

    Sitting in my grandmother's front room, waiting on the limo's to come and take us to the funeral home, I noticed my grandmother's eyes signaling for me to step into the kitchen for some one on one time. I pulled her chair out and she sat down slowly. Too slowly for my liking so I asked her, "You alright granny?" As I took the chair opposite hers.
"Not really son, but I'm a make it. Having to bury my grandchild ain't making it no better.
I been staying steady for Rhonda's sake, to give her a shoulder, but every time I'm alone for any amount of time, I cries my eyes out baby. Just thinking about my precious girls last minutes of life and how scared she must have been. She took a piece of my heart when she left here. But do you know

RESPECT REVENGE Pt. 1
"When Naptown Couldn't Sleep"

what would absolutely kill me?"
 Before I could even answer or respond at all, she continued.
"If something happened to you son. You are granny's pride and joy and always have been.
I pray and plead the blood of Jesus over you every night, that he encamps his angels round about you and watch over you. Not only for your sake, but for mines. Do you hear me?"

Hearing her talk like that, stripped me of all the hardness, tough guy, and street nigga I had become. I just put my head on the table and cried like a baby. I cried harder than I think I ever had in my life. I cried for Keisha and the loss of her life. I cried for my father. I cried for what auntie must be going through with the loss of her only child, but most of all, I think I cried for what I knew was to come.

As I got my emotions in check and my tears under control, I noticed that during my much needed cry, granny had come around to my side of the table and was rubbing my back as I let it out. She was, and had always been our rock. The foundation on which our family was built and she'd known I needed to release that or as she told me later, it would come out when I least expected it to.

I went through the funeral in zombie mode really. Seeing lil cuz laid up there in that casket seemed surreal to me. She was so full of life and had so much ahead of her, but had gotten clipped so young and so far, before her time, that it made me question God. Why her? Why now? My old man had taken it hard and it seemed to jar his mind a lil bit. He had been by auntie's side every step of the way and had been clean for the entire 5-day process. He was assigned pallbearer duties and was on the opposite of the casket and even though we were doing the unthinkable, (burying the baby of the family), it felt good to have my pops standing up and being counted for as a man in

RESPECT REVENGE Pt. 1
"When Naptown Couldn't Sleep"

this family. The family gathered back at granny's once we left the burial site to eat and reminisce how black folks do after funerals. I sat on the front porch and just thought about all I had done and all that I had been through. But what kept coming to the forefront of my thoughts was what I had to do now. It was time to push it, turn it up to a new level. I had the finances and resources to go to war. All that was missing was for me to push the button. I picked up my phone and hit P.U. He answered on the 2nd ring.

"What's up fam'?"
"I'm good my nigga. Get the guys together and meet me out at your spot in 2 hours, cool?" "I got you. Say no more. Anything else?"
"Tell them it's time to clear their calendars for a while cause we at it 24/7 until this shit is
done."
With that, I hung up and went in to say my good-bye's to the family.

RESPECT REVENGE Pt. 1
"When Naptown Couldn't Sleep"

CHAPTER
20

Over the next couple of weeks, we caught and killed nine of them get money niggas', but we couldn't' draw Money's bitch ass out for nothing. Then I got a very unexpected phone call from a very un-expected source. I answered my phone after 3 rings.
"Hello?"
"So you wanna beef wit the nigga who put you in the game huh?"
I said, "Who is this?" (knowing exactly who it was.)
"This Money nigga! You know who it is!"
"Fam', I don't know what you gettin' at, but come and meet me and we can talk in person. I don't like talking on these phones."
He said, "Nigga fuck you! I'm a be at you, you can believe that! Oh yeah, you put your lil cousin in a hell of a position didn't you. When Rico first started messing with her a while back, I told him that you probably put her on him. But I'll bet her dying wasn't part of the plan was it?"
After he said that, he laughed and hung up. I saved his number in my phone, because I would soon be making a call

RESPECT REVENGE Pt. 1
"When Naptown Couldn't Sleep"

of my own. I had met this little broad a couple of weeks back while I was out and about. She was into real estate and starting up small businesses. She had told me to give her a call if I was ever in the market for a house or a wife. I had told her that I had a girl, but baby was feeling a nigga, so she slipped me her business card. I wasn't looking for a wife but I had a little business to throw her way. I called her up and set up an appointment to meet her for lunch.

We met at a little outside cafe in the business district downtown. She had on a nice navy blue business suit, with the skirt stopping well above her knee's, but it still gave her a classy look. She was about 5 foot 4, light skinned, with shoulder length, jet black hair that she wore in a wrap style. She had on some gold wire frame glasses that made her look educated, but sexy at the same time. She walked up to the table where I was seated and I stood to shake her hand. When we met, she had introduced herself as Ty and even though her card had her full name on it, she felt it was necessary to formally introduce herself.

I'm Tyesha Davis."
I said, "I'm Eric." And I just left it at that.
I told her that I was on the hunt for a three-bedroom house in one of the surrounding counties, outside of the city. I told her that I would like to spend cash, without having the FED's crawling down my neck.
"Mr. Hunt, what you are asking me to do is illegal."
"Well, if you can't help me, then I'll just keep looking, sorry for was ting your time." I got up to leave and she stopped me.
"Wait, hold on a minute. Give me a few days and I'll see what I can do. We may be able to   work something out."
We shook hands and she said she would call me soon. Tyesha called me exactly two days later and told me to meet her in her downtown office. I arrived an hour later and the receptionist

RESPECT REVENGE Pt. 1
"When Naptown Couldn't Sleep"

told me she would only be a few moments, so I sat in a chair and waited.

After a five-minute wait, she opened her office door and waved me in.

"Good afternoon Mr. Hunt." She said while giving me a firm shake.

"Afternoon, but you can call me Eric."

"Okay Eric, listen. I may have found what you are looking for. I have this house in Greenwood that the bank has foreclosed on. If you pay the back taxes, which is only $6,500, I can probably get the bank to sell it to you for $160,000. But then that just leads us to another problem. We can't just walk in and close on a house with that kind of cash, so this is what we will do. I have people with good credit that I will have apply for a loan at the same bank. They will get approved, we purchase the house with the loan, then just pay the mortgage monthly. You pay me in one year increments, and I'll take care of everything. My fee's for these services will be $10,000 cash. So you get a $240,000-dollar house for, let me see ...$176,500 dollars even."

I just sat back and smiled because shorty knew her shit. She had made my day with her help, and she was looking more attractive to me by the minute.

One month later, I moved Granny, Trasheen, and Baby Eric to Greenwood and got them all settled in. Now that I had my family secured, I didn't have any weaknesses for none of these bitch ass niggas' to use against me. I was ready to make this hoe ass nigga Money come out of hiding ...

RESPECT REVENGE Pt. 1
"When Naptown Couldn't Sleep"

CHAPTER 21

The homicide dicks had turned up the heat in the hood and had a nigga laying low a lil bit. Then one day they came through and snatched up Cookie Face and Lil Lucky. I figured they would be out in 72 hours, once the police realized that they didn't have enough evidence to go to trial with. That was how shit usually went. I sent an attorney down town immediately to find out what the holdup was. He called me later that day and told me that on the day in question, 4 black males came off of the side of two houses on west 23rd St. (A block that was run by Money.) Two were armed with assault rifles, the other two with hand guns. They unloaded on a group of eight dudes. 4 were killed, 2 were critically wounded, and the other got away with only grazes. The police had no cooperating witnesses, and no suspects. Then someone came forward with information leading to the arrest of Cookie and Lucky. He said he wouldn't' t know the name of the informant until they were formally charged and received their probable cause affidavits. He said he would call as soon as he knew more. I told him to be expecting my girl at his office in the morning with some money.

RESPECT REVENGE Pt. 1
"When Naptown Couldn't Sleep"

I sent Sheen down there the following morning with $40,000 cash for the lawyer and had her drop a stack on each of their books. I knew exactly the night that the lawyer was talking about because I was one of the four dudes in black. It was me, Cookie, Lil Smurf, and Lil Lucky. We had been turning up the heat on them niggas' blocks every night and had hit the jackpot when them niggas' thought it was cool to curb serve on the block. They haven't been out there ever since. Them blocks were like a ghost town now, waiting on me and mine's to set up shop once this drama shit was over with.

    I called Lil Smurf for a whole day once I found out what went down with Cookie and Lucky, to tell him to lay low, but I couldn't reach him. I started to think that maybe Money had snatched him up or something, it wasn't like my man to not be able to be reached, especially when I called. I hoped he was a'ight ....

RESPECT REVENGE Pt. 1
"When Naptown Couldn't Sleep"

CHAPTER 22

Money started to realize that he had lost too much ground and too many men in this beef we had going on. He knew that he if he didn't make something happen quick, he would have to go ahead and fold or we were bound to get him. Don't forget, Money was a Hard-Part nigga too and quitting wasn't in his blood; so he called in some reinforcements.

He had done a five-year FED bid from the time he was 19 until he was 24 and that's why I had never met him prior to me getting out of Boys school. While he was locked up, he had become a Sunni Muslim and was jammed tight with some GD's out of Chicago who were also practicing Muslims. One in particular, they called Y.G., but he went by his Muslim name which was Abdul Gaffar. He was a known head buster, and jumped at the cash that Money offered him to come down from the Chi and help him solve his problems. Abdul Gaffar also brought two of his own killers with him. They were Muslims too, and they wore the big beards and all, but they were strapped to the teeth. I got a chance to see their work almost instantly ...

I had been laying back with one of my lil females,

RESPECT REVENGE Pt. 1
"When Naptown Couldn't Sleep"

when I got a call from some of the soldiers in the hood.

"Man, they found two bodies in a car around on Burton Ave.! Police everywhere and we don' t know who it is cause they haven't pulled em' out yet!"

I said, "A'ight my dude, keep me posted, I'll be through there in a minute."

I jumped in my latest lil whip, a "96" Chevy Impala SS., and smashed towards the hood.

I pulled up 15 minutes later and they were just getting ready to pull whoever it was out and put em' in body bags. Burton Ave. was a street in my hood where everyone hung out and got drunk or high. We sold a little dope over there, but mainly it was just a chill spot. When the police pulled the driver out, it fucked me up off top. It was O.G. Vester, Falcon's right hand man. Whoever killed him, had done a number on him, cause from what I could see, most of his fingers were missing and his face looked like raw hamburger meat. Somebody had taken a straight razor to my man something serious. I knew once I seen O.G. Vester, that the other dude in the car could be none other than Falcon Eddie. My suspicions were confirmed when they pulled him out and his hands were duct taped behind his back and his throat was slit from ear to ear. These niggas were straight killas', and whoever had gotten to them had not got them with a gun, but up close and personal. As the homicide detectives finished up the scene, this big black one, the same one that had locked up Lucky and Cookie, started whispering to his partner and looking my way. I mugged on em' for a second, then turned around and faded into the crowd. P.U. called my phone and told me he was on Ms. Jones porch and asked me to step over there for a second.

Ms. Jones was the nosiest woman in the world. If something was shaking on Burton Ave. she knew about it. She

RESPECT REVENGE Pt. 1
"When Naptown Couldn't Sleep"

sat on her porch all day and night; drank beer, swatted fly's, and watched everything coming and going. She had been living there for about 20 years and knew everybody and all they business too. When I walked up on the porch, she was all smiles.
    "Hey E, how you been baby? I ain' t seen you in forever."
    "I'm good M s. Jones, how you been?"
"I'm fine, just trying to mind mine's and stay out the way."
We both knew that was so far from the truth.
 I said, "What's up P.U.?" He looked at Ms. Jones and said, "Tell him what you told me Auntie." She took it from there.
    "Well, I'd say it was about 5:30 or 6:00 this morning, I don't know why I could not sleep, so I got up and started watching T.V. I fixed me a little breakfast and was waiting for the liquor store to open, cause I'm fresh out of beer. Well, I stepped out on the porch and seen that same car they just pulled them folks out of and it stopped right where it is at now. They stayed in there for about 10 minutes, then a white truck pulled up beside it and two men with them big beards got out and climbed in the truck they even had them funny little hats on their heads. Well the truck turned and came back my way and that's when I saw the driver. I even tried to wave at him."
    I said, "Who was it Ms. Jones?"
"Money was driving the truck. I know everybody at odds with the boy, but he ain't never done nothing to me. But once they pulled Vester and Falcon out that car, I felt like I had to tell somebody."
So I asked her, "Who else you tell Ms. Jones?"
    She said, "Just P.U. and now you."
I told her to keep it at that and peeled off four one-hundred-dollar bill's and handed them to her.
    "Aw baby, you don't have to do that."
 But before she could even finish saying it she had grabbed them and was stuffing them down her bra.

RESPECT REVENGE Pt. 1
"When Naptown Couldn't Sleep"

I wasn't upset because the two O.G.'s were dead, they were Gangsta's, and Gangta's died in the streets, it happens. But for Money to slide through the hood with his new hitters and get two of the best, then leave them for everybody to see, he made me realize that it was time to bring this shit to a head, one way or the other. I needed to do something to make him make a mistake, so I could go ahead and checkmate this nigga, once and for all ...

RESPECT REVENGE Pt. 1
"When Naptown Couldn't Sleep"

CHAPTER 23

The next morning, I got a call from the lawyer, he said, "I got the paper work after the boys were charged today. Seems to me whoever this person is, had intimate knowledge of the situation. He needed to get himself out of a jam that he got caught up in, and use this case to free himself. He was pulled over one night a couple of months back and got caught with 9oz of coke and a .45 caliber handgun. He was facing a lot of time, and told the arresting officer that he knew something that the homicide officers would be interested in. When they got him downtown, they cut him a deal and he spilled his guts. Do you know a Lamont Young?"
When he said that I damn near dropped the phone.
He said, "Are you there?"
"Yeah I'm here."
"So I take it you know him?"
"Yeah I know him."
"Well, their whole case hinges on his testimony, without it, they have nothing."
I said, "Okay thanks and I'll be at you soon."
"Okay Eric, take care buddy."

RESPECT REVENGE Pt. 1
"When Naptown Couldn't Sleep"

"Yeah I will." And with that I hung up.
I couldn't believe this nigga Lil Smurf had flipped and turned rat like that. He knows he could have come to me and I would have had a top flight lawyer looking for holes in his case to get that shit threw out on a technicality. See the thing about a state case, they disappeared as quickly as they appeared. I now understood why I hadn't been hearing from my man, or he hadn't been answering his phone. He had a dirty little secret. But I know the dumb nigga like I know the back of my hand. He only had two places outside the hood where he went or even could go. His baby momma had a place out south, and he had a stripper bitch that he loved on the eastside. I was gonna hate to do it, but I was gonna have to reach out and touch my comrad because a rat don't deserve no breaks. I didn't plan on letting the love that I had for this nigga cloud my judgment one bit….

RESPECT REVENGE Pt. 1
"When Naptown Couldn't Sleep"

CHAPTER 24

I decided that the time was now to bring Money up out of the bushes. When you use to hang with a nigga the way me and Money use to hang, you tend to learn a lot about a mufucka'. Shit that can be used against him if ever necessary, right now it was necessary. That is the reason I moved my family out of bounds, to eliminate all unnecessary weaknesses. Money's mother had died when he was young, from Cancer. After that his pops turned to alcohol real bad, but kept a job and a roof over he and Money's head. Money had taken me over his father's crib many times when we were still hanging, but he hadn't thought to move him to protect him while we was at war. So I figured I would make Money's emotions his motivation, by hitting him where I knew it would hurt. Mr. Coleman stayed on the Eastside of town, on a street called Tacoma. He had a nice little ranch style house, with a nice green lawn, and a porch that he liked to sit on and listen to Jazz, while he sipped on Crown Royal.

He knew me by name and face, so it didn't startle him one bit when me and P.U. walked up on his porch and helped ourselves to a seat on his patio furniture.

RESPECT REVENGE Pt. 1
"When Naptown Couldn't Sleep"

I said, "Hey Mr. Coleman, what's been up with you?"
"Hey Lil E, how you been? I ain't seen you in a while."
"I been just chillin', trying to maintain and stay out of trouble."
He said, "I doubt that, you and Money probably raising plenty hell on that Westside."
"Naw, not us. Speaking of Money, he told me to meet him over here."
Mr. Coleman said, "I told that boy don't be setting up no meetings over here. He was by here yesterday with three sneaky lookin' jokers, all of them wearing kufi's and beards. He talking bout they some of his buddies from Chicago, they came down to party. I told him to take em' where the party at then, don't bring em' over here!"

    I looked at P.U. and1 we both knew that he had bought them dudes down from Chi-town for one reason and one reason only, and it was not to party.
So I said, "Mr. Coleman, can I use your phone real quick to call Money?"
He got up and went into the house to get the phone and we were right behind him. Once we got in the house, P.U. shut and locked the door. Mr. Coleman heard the door shut and turned and looked at me.
"What's goin' on E?" I only had one answer for him.
"War Mr. Coleman, and I'm sorry, but you just became a causality of it."
Then I kicked his legs out from under him.
I didn't want to fire no guns because these neighbors out here were nosy, and I couldn't afford the police to come just yet. So I pulled out my .45 and just started pistol whippin' his ass.

    I pistol whipped him with all the rage and frustration that had built up over the loss of my loved ones. I literally blacked out on old school. I felt his son was directly responsible for all this

RESPECT REVENGE Pt. 1
"When Naptown Couldn't Sleep"

mess. His jealousy and greed made him kill Big June over some chicken scratch, which I felt lead to the death of Keisha, which made me have to move my family. Fuck Money! Everything he stood for! And everybody he loved!

By the time P.U. grabbed my arm and told me that the old man was gone, I was covered in blood and so were the walls. From the neck up, he looked like a plate of spaghetti. I picked him up and sat him on the couch in front of the T.V. and turned it on. Then I picked up my cell phone and scrolled down the phonebook, stopping on the entry I had labeled "Snake" and pressed send. Money picked up on the second ring, "What you want bitch ass nigga'?" He knew it was me.

I said, "I got bored from not seeing you for a while, then you got my attention with the gift you and your Muslim buddies left me in the hood, so I decided to go and see pops Coleman. We was watching the news together, and talkin' bout how the Westside done went to shit, with all the violence and what not. Then he just fell asleep and I can't wake him up, so you might want to check on him. Oh yeah, remember what you said about Keisha being a sacrifice? I guess you never thought about the position you left pops in huh?" Then I hung up.

RESPECT REVENGE Pt. 1
"When Naptown Couldn't Sleep"

CHAPTER 25

I knew that where ever he was, he was gonna stop what he was doing and fly over here like a bat out of hell. By doing so, he would be falling right into my trap.

Me and P.U. had choppers in the trunk of the Ford Taurus we had parked down the street. I had a Mack 90, and so did he. P.U. was laying in some bushes directly across the street from the old man's crib. I was laid beside a car that was in the driveway of the house next door. As we waited, all sorts of thoughts went through my mind. This shit could come to an end right here tonight or I could possibly lose my life. Whichever way it went, I would find out soon, because I heard an engine roaring, coming flying down the street. All of a sudden, a big white Suburban came to a screeching halt in front of pops crib, and before it could even come to a complete stop, Money was out of the passenger side and running towards the house. As if he read my mind, P.U. started lettin' loose wit the chopper. It sounded like New Year's Eve out that bitch! I could see the fire coming from the end of the weapon, and the Burban was rockin' side to side like they had switches on that bitch. Right when Money

RESPECT REVENGE Pt. 1
"When Naptown Couldn't Sleep"

made it to the door, he turned and got low, trying to avoid being caught in the ambush. It caused him to take his attention off of his surroundings, and I let my chopper holla his way in rapid succession. He did a bear crawl on into the house and slammed the door shut with his foot.

Just then, the driver door of the truck flew open and a stocky brown skinned older guy, with a white kufi and a grey beard, rolled out and started firing a Mack 10 in P.U.'s direction. He was clutching his stomach with one hand, and squeezing off rounds with the other. He screamed out "ALLAHU AKBAR! ALLAHU AKBAR!" (which I guess was praise to his God) then charged P.U. steady firing. P.U. came up out of the bushes, and the two exchanged bullets like some shit straight out of a movie. I charged the old Gangsta from behind and when he fell, I put five rounds from my chopper into his torso. His eyes were wide open, but he was staring at nothing. Whatever he had said to Allah, I hope it was heard because he was in route to meet his maker. I got to P.U., who was on his stomach, gasping for air. I rolled him over and knew immediately that he wouldn't make it. He was breathing like a fish out of water, he had blood coming from everywhere, and then all of a sudden, I smelled shit. I knew that when a person released their bowels, death was at their doorstep. He was trying to say something, so I put my ear to his lips. Through the gurgling blood, I made out,

"Finish what we started, get that nigga' Money."
Just when he was saying that, the nigga Money came flying out of the front door of his father's crib blazing something heavy in my direction. Dirt was flying up all around me, so I dove for cover behind a car parked at the curb, and returned fire with my .45. One of his rounds came through the window of the car and got me in the shoulder. I stopped firing for a second to check my wound and then I heard "Click-Click -Click."

RESPECT REVENGE Pt. 1
"When Naptown Couldn't Sleep"

Money had ran out of bullets, but didn't realize it because he was in a blind rage from finding his father in such a condition. I jumped up, letting my hand cannon bark
"Boom! Boom! Boom!"
Money turned to run because 2 of my shots found their mark. The next one hit him in the back of the leg and he fell hard on his face, then began trying to crawl on his stomach, but I had his ass now. I walked up and kicked his bitch ass in his ribs, causing him to cry out in pain and turn over at the same time. I looked him in the eye and asked him,
"Do you know why nigga?"
He said, "Yeah I know why. Because your bitch ass always wanted to be me!"
 It fucked me up that this dumb ass nigga still thought it was a secret that he had killed the big homie.
I said, "Naw, that ain't the case, I never wanted to be you, I was cool with bein' the little homie, but that's where we differ huh? You couldn't accept playin your position, so you killed the leader of the team."
He finally had a look of recognition on his face, like it all made sense now. I guess he thought he had gotten away, but he was wrong.
"Boom! Boom!
I hit him with my last two rounds in his face. I thought it would feel good when I finally killed Money, but look at all that I had lost on the way ...
I turned in P.U. 's direction to check and see if he was alive, and just like I figured, he wasn't.
 I heard sirens in the distance and they were getting closer quick, so I made my way to the Ford Taurus and got behind the wheel. My fuckin' shoulder was killing me. It didn't hurt as bad when my adrenalin was pumping, but now that bitch was

RESPECT REVENGE Pt. 1
"When Naptown Couldn't Sleep"

throbbin'. I turned around in someone's driveway and crept off down one of the back streets. This war was officially over, but look at the price I paid. I was lucky to be alive because so many of' us weren't.

RESPECT REVENGE Pt. 1
"When Naptown Couldn't Sleep"

CHAPTER 26

I had to get to the hospital because I was bleeding pretty bad, but I didn't know who to call. I couldn't go to an area hospital because I knew the police would be there lookin' for anyone checking in with fresh gunshot wounds. I flipped open my phone and I don't know why, but I called the real estate chick, Tyesha. She answered after four rings,
    "Hello."
    I said, "I need your help."
    "Who is this?"
"This is Eric. Listen, I've been shot and can't go to the hospital and I didn't know who else to call."
She said "Where are you?"
I told her, "Meet me at the corner of 30th and Sherman Dr., in the parking lot of the 7-11 store. I'm in a red Ford Taurus."
"Okay, give me ten minutes, I'm not far away!"
She pulled up eight minutes later in a Cadillac STS. I got out of the Taurus and hopped in with her. She helped me into the front seat and I could see the panic in her eyes.
"Oh my God! Are you okay?!"
""Yeah, I'm cool. Just get me out of here."

RESPECT REVENGE Pt. 1
"When Naptown Couldn't Sleep"

She took off heading west, like she had a destination in mind. So I asked her,
      "Where are you headed?"
 "Just relax, save your strength, I got you."
I got on the phone and called one of my lil partners in the hood and told him to go get the Taurus and burn it up. My blood was all over it, and I couldn't afford for the police to stumble up on that. He said he was on it right away and I hung up and laid my head back on the head rest.
When I woke up, I was in a hospital bed with bandages on my shoulder and Tyesha was asleep in a chair beside my bed. I had no idea where I was at. I tried to move and a sharp pain shot through my whole left side. I hollered out in pain,
      "Ahh! Shit!"
Tyesha jumped up and helped to ease me back down onto my pillow.
      "Boy! Take it easy!"
      I asked "Where we at?"
"We are in Terre Haute Memorial Hospital."
Terre Haute was an hour outside of the city, and far enough away where Tyesha felt comfortable taking me too. She said,
"I rushed you here last night and they came and carried you in here and they treated your wound. I told them that we were out walking along the canal here in town, on a romantic date and two thugs tried to rob us and you tried to defend me and ended up shot."
I smiled as I listened to her tell me the story she had told the police, cause baby had plenty of game about herself. She said that I would be released later that day. Then she asked me,
"So what are you gonna do Eric?"
 "What do you mean?"
"I mean, you need rest and it seems to me that you may need to

RESPECT REVENGE Pt. 1
"When Naptown Couldn't Sleep"

lay low for a while. "
I said, "Yeah, I guess you're right. I'll probably go out to Greenwood and let my family take care of me for a while." I seen a disappointed look on her face. So I continued,
"Unless you had other plans for me?"
She said, "Well, I do have a 3-bedroom house up north by myself, and I have a guest room you could use at least until you get your strength back."

"I don't know; you might try to take advantage of me while I'm weak."
She looked at me with a smile on her face and said,
"Don't flatter yourself. I should be worried about having a Gangster under my roof."
The Doctor came in a few hours later and released me. He told me that I should give myself a week or two to give my body time to heal, and that only rest would do it. I agreed to stay with Tyesha because I did need rest and time to collect my thoughts and figure out my next move. Plus, I was feeling baby girl and I could tell that she was feeling me and I wanted to get to know her a little better....

RESPECT REVENGE Pt. 1
"When Naptown Couldn't Sleep"

CHAPTER 27

One week later, I was up and about, but I hadn't left Tyesha's crib. I was feeling about 75% which was good, being that one week earlier I had taken a .40 cal round straight through the shoulder. I had missed P.U.'s funeral because I knew that the homicide dicks would be there and I couldn't show up with this big ass bandage on my shoulder. I had sent Tyesha to sign the book and to get me an obituary. All the niggas' in the hood knew what went down by putting two and two together, so they kept me posted. Lil Smurf even showed up, with his police ass. I had one of my lil niggas' from the hood follow him to see where he was laying his head. He jumped straight on the highway and headed out south towards his baby's mamma's house. So now I knew where to reach out and touch him. I still had 11 bricks of coke left, 3 I had copped just prior to all the drama, plus the eight I had got from under Big June's dog house. Plus, I had about $200,000 on stash so I was a'ight being that I hadn't sold no dope in the six months since Big June got killed. It was time for me to set up shop and get some real money because I was now in control of the whole Hard-Part. When one controls the Hard-Part, one runs

RESPECT REVENGE Pt. 1
"When Naptown Couldn't Sleep"

the whole Westside. Then on top of that, I now had a plug in Jake, Big June's older brother, that would allow me to sow up my whole side of town.

I had the power and respect, now it was time for me to get the money. But before I could do any of that, I had to get my muscle out of jail, and the only thing stopping that was Lil Smurf.

      I rested and chilled with Tyesha for two more weeks. We went out to eat and rented movies almost every night. I was really starting to feel baby girl. We made love one night and it was like we had been together many times before, the way our bodies meshed and how we took our time and made sure the other was satisfied. She had me by five years, I was 21 and she was 26, but we got it on like we had been made for each other. After we had finished making love, we laid in each other's arms and she told me how she felt.

"Look Eric, I haven't had many relationships because I've been pushing myself through school and working on my career, so I haven't had time to be fucking with no nothing ass niggas'. But I have fallen for you and I've fallen hard. From the first time I met you for lunch, I knew I wanted to get to know you better, and now that I have, I want to keep you all to myself. I know that's not possible because I have to share you with the streets, but all I ask of you is that you be careful and that you be good to me. If you do that, then I'm 100% with you. I realize the risk of loving a bad boy, but I'm willing to take that chance. With you getting money and me being into real estate, we could clean up some of that money, and be straight in no time. Let's just take it one day at a time, but please don't break my heart okay?"

I loved the fact that baby was so honest about her feelings for a nigga, she knew what she wanted in a career and she went out and got it. She knew what she wanted in a man, and she was definitely making her move, I respected that. I told her,

RESPECT REVENGE Pt. 1
"When Naptown Couldn't Sleep"

"Look, I 've been hustlin' since I was a shorty, and the money been cool, but I'm gettin' ready to come into some real money. If you are real wit me, then I'm a be real wit you. I need a woman who knows her position and knows how to play it. If you can do that then the sky is the limit for us."

She said, "Well, then I 'm yours."

And with that she kissed me on the lips then slid down and made love to my dick with her mouth ...

RESPECT REVENGE Pt. 1
"When Naptown Couldn't Sleep"

CHAPTER 28

I called the hood and had two of my guys give me updates on shit. They said everything was all good and they had been maintaining by copping work from another hustler from the hood named Harvey. I had my lil niggas' meet me at this lil apartment that I was renting on the Westside, not far from the hood. Brian, who we called B-Boy, and his little brother Kev, had been hustlin' wit us for a while now. These lil niggas were straight up block burners, they hustled 24/7 and pulled all-nighters damn near every night. I sat them both down and said,

"Listen, I'm a give ya'll two of these bricks so ya'll can get shit started again out there. I want ya'll to cook em' up raw and break one down into eightballs, quarters, and half ounces. Break the other one down into dimes, dubs, and fifties. Ya'll take 26th street and Roache block. Them the two best blocks in the hood. On one of em', get it jumping with the fiends and shit. The other, I want ya'll pushing the balls, quarters and halves. Then give 25th street and Edgemont Ave. to the other young hustlers. Front them work and let them get their blocks bumpin'. That way we got the four

RESPECT REVENGE Pt. 1
"When Naptown Couldn't Sleep"

inner blocks in the hood back jumpin'. That will leave 2 blocks on either side, plus the corner and the three main streets that run in opposite directions of ya'lls blocks. I'm a turn the last block at each end of the hood into security blocks, that way we know exactly who is coming and going."
After I finished talking, my two lil niggas' had this look in their eyes that told me that they was feeling the way I'd laid my plans out and the vision I had for the hood. They left with the two bricks, one to get their block pumping, the other to feed the lil niggas in the hood. See, if you feed the wolves, then the pack would stay together, but if you left some hungry, then they would turn on each other out of the need to survive. Now that that was done and over with, I had to get my mans' an em' out, so I jumped on the freeway and headed to the Southside to holla at my man Lil Smurf.
Lil Smurf was actually an easy nigga to find. I pulled up in his baby mamma's apartments and right there as big as day was my old Lexus, the one I had just not too long ago sold him. I parked a little ways down from it, and waited for the sun to set.
There were a couple of people coming and going, but it wasn't too much to where I had to abort my mission. I had a .44 Bulldog on me this night. This mufucka will take your head clean off of your shoulders. I got out of my under bucket and went and set off the alarm on the Lexus.
   "Beep! Beep! Beep! Beep! Beep!"
That shit was loud as hell. 30 seconds later, Smurf came rushing out the door with the remote in hand to turn off the alarm. I came off the side of the car that was parked beside the Lexus.
"What's up Lil Smurf?"
It looked like he saw a fuckin' ghost.
   "Hey, what's up Lil E, What you doin' out here?"
I said, "I was gonna ask you the same thang."

RESPECT REVENGE Pt. 1
"When Naptown Couldn't Sleep"

"Man, I just been out here chillin', It been way too much goin' on in the hood lately."

"I can understand that, but why you ain't been answering your phone?"

He said, "You know how them hoe's is when your phone keeps ringing, I be cuttin' it off so I don't have to hear Crystal's mouth."

I looked him in the eye and said,

"Why did you do it Lil Smurf?"

"Do what my nigga?"

I snapped, "Stop playin wit me nigga! You know what the fuck I'm talking about!"

With that, I pulled out the .44 Bulldog and cocked the hammer. He broke right down.

"Man, Fuck them nigga's! They ain't shit, you see I ain't tell on you. It used to be about just me and you and then they came and just fazed me out! Plus, them people had me E, talking bout 20 years. I couldn't go out like that!"

He had tears in his eyes. This nigga made me want to throw up, how the fuck can you justify being a fuckin' rat! Fuck that! When you get in them streets, you know the consequences, live with it, or stay on the porch. It hurt my heart because I use to love this nigga. But I couldn't tolerate this shit here. I pointed my strap at his face and he looked me in the eye with this pleading look,

"So you just gonna kill me now?"

I said, "Naw, you killed yourself!"

Then I let my dog bark one time, sending Lil Smurf to wherever rats go when their deeds finally catch up to em'.

I got out of there and felt kind of bad for the way things turned out for Lil Smurf, but it is what it is.

RESPECT REVENGE Pt. 1
"When Naptown Couldn't Sleep"

Three days later, the lawyer called and said that the prosecutor had faxed him the motion to dismiss on the grounds of a lack of evidence, and that Lucky and Cookie would be released later that night. I called Tyesha and told her to rent out the biggest club in the city because we were throwing a welcome home party on Saturday night.

RESPECT REVENGE Pt. 1
"When Naptown Couldn't Sleep"

CHAPTER
29

It was Wednesday night when I sat in front of the county jail in my black on black "98 Tahoe. Me and Tyesha had been out there for over an hour. Then the door flew open and my niggas' came walking out with the Jew that we had for a lawyer. I got out and greeted the group.
"What' s up my niggas?" Cookie answered first,
"What's up E, Good to see yo ass!"
He hugged and dapped me up. Then Lil Lucky grabbed a nigga tight and said,
"What's up family, how you been out here?"
This nigga just walked out of the county jail, and he worried about how I'm doing.
I said, "I'm good fam, I'm just happy to see my mans' an em' free again! I had no doubt, I knew how it would turn out, it was just a matter of time."
The lawyer cleared his throat and told me if I needed him then I knew what to do. I introduced him to Ty, (that was Tyesha' s nick name.)
"Silverstein, this is Tyesha. Tyesha, Silverstein."
They exchanged pleasantries and he went on his way. He

RESPECT REVENGE Pt. 1
"When Naptown Couldn't Sleep"

jumped in a brand new Dodge Viper and smoked his tires up on the way out of there. Lucky looked at it and got excited.
He said, "I got to get me one of them!" We jumped in the truck and rolled out.
I reached under the front passenger seat cause Ty was driving, and pulled out twin .45 Glocs and handed them over the seat to my guys.
　　"Welcome home Gangsta's"
Cookie said, "It feels good to be here, layin' in that mufucka gets old quick!"
As we were talking, an all-white Crown Victoria, with the light on the dash jumped behind us and hit his lights.
"Whoop! Whoop!"
We pulled to the side of the road and the same big black cop who had been on the scene of Falcon's and O.G. Vesters murder, plus had locked up Cookie and Lucky, walked up to the driver's window. He stuck his whole head into the car, disregarding Ty, and looked at the three of us.
　　He said, "I want you to know who I am! I am E. Young. I already know who you are Lil E. I know you were there when Money and his father were killed. You left P.U. out there. I know you had something to do with that situation with Rico on the Eastside. You left your little cousin out there. And, I know you are responsible for the drama that's going on, on the Westside. But what really pisses me off is that I know you killed your own friend to save these two pieces of shit. You usually leave something behind, but you never
leave me nothing I can use. When you do, I'm a bury yo funky ass, you hear me! I'm on your back like a cheap suit! You can believe that! When I do get you, you will be gone for good!"
I looked him in the eye and said,
"I believe you officer, but until then, don't talk to me, talk to my

RESPECT REVENGE Pt. 1
"When Naptown Couldn't Sleep"

lawyer."

I handed him Silverstein's card, then told Ty to pull off. He was hot as fish grease, but I ain't give a fuck, I had money to get.

I gave my nigga's a bankroll and told them to get fly on Saturday night, we had something planned. We dropped them off over each of their girlfriends houses and told them to be easy until the weekend came.

Me and Ty headed out to her house to count out the money I had collected from B-Boy, Lil Kev and Harvey. See, after I had done business with B-Boy and Lil Kev, I called Harvey up, the nigga they had been copping weight from while I was out of business. I told Harvey that I respected his hustle and because he was from the hood, I was offering him a position in the new Hard-Part. I let him know that if any dope get sold in the hood, then it got to be coming through me. I had fought and killed for these blocks, so if a nigga wasn't with me then he was against me, and niggas' ain't want them type of problems. So I gave Harvey five of the nine bricks that I had left, and told him how it would go. After we got back what I had invested in each brick, then we would split the profit 50/50. So he gave me $20,000 for each brick, plus $6,000 of the $12,00. profit. We were making $32,400 per brick because we were letting all the dope in the hood go for the same price. Half oz was $450.00, ounces were $900.00. He could only sell half oz's on up, that was his lane and I told him to stay in it. That way B Boy and Lil Kev could sell 10's, 20 s and 50's on their blocks, serve the lil niggas eight-balls and quarters, and the rest of the nigga's in the hood could cop from Harvey. Now, I could focus on anything from 4 ounces, to the whole loaf. But pretty soon, all
of that would change, because it was time to holla at Jake …

RESPECT REVENGE Pt. 1
"When Naptown Couldn't Sleep"

CHAPTER 30

Saturday night was here and we couldn't wait to get it poppin' off in the Mecca. The Mecca was the biggest, baddest club in the city. This mufucka held well over 1,000 people. It had 3 bars and 3 dance floors, plus a V.I.P that was off the chain. The V.I.P itself was separated from the rest of the club by a big ass glass window in the shape of a dollar sign. It had couches and love seats along the walls, with its very own dance floor in the middle, plus a bar of its own. Anybody who was anybody from the whole Westside was up in that bitch. Everybody was dressed to impress and niggas' jewelry game was sick. Outside looked like a fuckin' car show. When me, Cookie and Lucky walked in the door, the D.J. gave us much love.

"Oh shit! It's them Hard-Part nigga's! Some of the realest young nigga's in the city! What's up Gangstas!"

We walked through that mufucka like we owned that bitch. We had fought from the ground up to enjoy life, and I felt like we should start enjoying it that very night. Ty stayed home, cause the club wasn't her scene, but she had put the whole thang together for me. We were greeted like stars,

RESPECT REVENGE Pt. 1
"When Naptown Couldn't Sleep"

dapps and hugs from every where. You could feel the love coming from the streets. Plus, the baddest hoe's in the city was off in there wearing next to nothing.

We told the waitress in the V.I.P to hit us all off with bottles of Moet and we popped tops huddled around the table. Me and my two niggas'. We was celebrating their release, but we were also celebrating the beginning of the good life. They still didn't know about the bricks I had come across from under the dog house, nor did they know about the new connect.

I had the main niggas from every hood on the Westside that we didn't have no problems with, off in V.I.P. I had been sliding down on them one by one, letting them know that my numbers were $3,000 less than what they were paying now, and I was getting ready to bring the love to the Westside. The going rate was $25,000 a brick, but being that Jake had already told me that the ticket would be $16,000 per kilo, I could sell em' for $22,000 apiece and still make $6,000 profit per loaf.

After I finished making my rounds, I settled in a booth in the back next to the man who would be responsible for these magic numbers.

"Jake, what's up my dude?"

He said, "What's up my guy? I see you got the west in here deep tonight!"

"Yeah, my men just got out, plus I'm celebrating the beginning of a new day."

He answered, "I feel you my dude. Listen, I want you to meet my man Juan-C. He originally from Beechwood projects, but he done took over the whole eastside with the numbers he got on that work. He is my eastside rep, and you just became the west. See, I got the whole city basically. I'm responsible for 85% of the cocaine that move through here. You got a few independent dudes that are movin' major weight, but they just in

RESPECT REVENGE Pt. 1
"When Naptown Couldn't Sleep"

the way."
Juan-C was a tall dark skinned nigga with dreads. He carried himself like he had that paper. I didn't take him for no killer, but he had hustler written all over him. Jake made the introductions, "Juan-C, this is Big E. Big E, this is Juan-C."

We shook hands and then he excused himself from the table. I felt a bad vibe off of the dude. He acted like he had something on his mind the way he just got up and rolled out. Jake looked at me and said,

"You getting ready to be one of the heaviest in the city, ain't nothing little about you no more. You ain't Lil E no more, You Big E now!"

This cat reminded me so much of the homie Big June. June had groomed me to the corner hustlin' and home invasion game, even the murder game, but this nigga Jake was gettin' ready to help me take this shit to a whole new level. Jake was ready to roll out, and he handed me a phone and told me to hang on to it. Then he said,

"In order for us to stay out here in these streets, we got to be smart. That phone there is just for me and you. I'm a call you Tuesday morning so we can get this shit crackin'. Oh yeah, I like how you turned this mufucka upside down about Big June. That was real shit right there."

And with that, him and Juan-C rolled out.

We partied for the rest of the night and had a fucking ball. By 3:30 everybody was paired off with a bad bitch. Cookie and Lucky both had thick red-bones on their arms. We made our exit surrounded by Hard-Part goons. People fell in line when everybody was eating, and I was feeding the hood.

Once we got outside, there were two brand new Dodge Vipers parked nose to nose in front of the door. One black, the other one was red. They both had tinted windows.

RESPECT REVENGE Pt. 1
"When Naptown Couldn't Sleep"

I went in my pocket and pulled out two sets of keys and tossed them to my niggas'. Lucky flew to the red one and revved his engine up. I looked at both of em' and said,
 "Welcome back baby! Now let's get this money!"

RESPECT REVENGE Pt. 1
"When Naptown Couldn't Sleep"

CHAPTER 31

I got home to Ty about 30 minutes later, she was on the couch watching T.V. when I walked in.
I said, "What's up baby, what you doin' up?"
"What you think I'm doin' up? I'm waitin' on my man."
I grabbed the remote and killed the T.V., then pulled her to me and kissed her with a lot of passion. I was fallin' in love with baby girl and it felt good. It seemed like everything was falling in place for a nigga. Good woman, the family was straight, I had a connect out of this world, plus I had crushed my enemies. I smiled and whispered in Ty's ear,
  "My dick is harder than a Chinese math problem."
 She laughed and said, "Yeah, but who is it hard for? Me or one of your little groupies from the club?"
  "Who did I rush home to give it to?"
She put her arms around my neck and set it off with some love from them soft ass lips of hers. I thought we was going to make it to the bedroom, but we went at it right there in the front room. I loved the way baby's eyes got dreamy when I kissed and sucked on her neck. I lifted her gown over her head and she had on a pink thong with the bra to match. Her

RESPECT REVENGE Pt. 1
"When Naptown Couldn't Sleep"

toe nails and finger nails were painted the exact same shade of pink. I unhooked her bra, freeing them pretty titties of hers with the perfect size brown nipples.
I showed them titties plenty of love, right there on the couch, going back and forth between the two. I raised up to take off my shirt and she wiggled out of that thong. Her pussy hairs were shaved low and neatly trimmed. Seeing that pretty pussy sent me from love making mode, to beast mode.   I stood straight up and snatched off my pants and boxers quick, and got down on my knees as she laid back on the couch watching me with anticipation. I pushed her legs back and told her to hold them right there, then I buried my face in her pretty lil pussy. I went at them lips like somebody told me I could kiss my bride, suckin' and lickin' in rhythm, driving baby girl crazy. I got hold of that clit and sucked on it gently, but with enough firmness to send her over the edge. She said,

"Ooh my God baby, what are you trying to do to me? I'm bout to cum!"
I told her, "Well then cum for me baby!"
That's all she needed to hear. She let out a moan from deep down in her belly, and then her pussy started contracting and she released her juices all over my face. The taste of her love drove me crazy. I told her to hold on to the back of the couch. She turned around and did it, arching her back up, thinking that I was about to hit it from the back. But seeing them pussy lips shinning from her juices, I had to have another taste, so I put my face in it and ate that thang from behind. I really sent her into a frenzy with my tongue game, and she begged me to put the pipe to her.

"Please, I need to feel you inside of me!"
I stood up and ran my hand up and down her pussy collecting as much of her wetness as I could, then stood back and stroked my dick while I just looked at this bad mufucka that was feening for

RESPECT REVENGE Pt. 1
"When Naptown Couldn't Sleep"

me to beat it up.

She said, "Come on baby, stop playing. Put it in."

So I eased up behind her and rubbed my joint up and down her pussy lips, then put the head in and gave her slow, shallow strokes. She was trying to back it up so the dick could fill her up, but I wouldn't let it. I waited until she reached between her legs and started stroking her own clit before I went at her with my best moves. Long, deep strokes, mixed in with short joints. Once we got in rhythm, she bit down on her bottom lip and held on to the back of the couch and I went to town on that pussy. You would have thought we were in front of a live studio audience with all the "Oohing" and "Aaghing" that was going on in the room. She felt me stiffen up, getting ready to let the baby's fly. So she hopped up and sat down on the couch in front of me and took my tool in her mouth and put her head game down somethin' serious. She took all I had to offer and then some. My legs got wobbly and I tried to pull my dick away once she had cleaned it up, but she wouldn't let it go. The sensation was too much for me to handle and I couldn't take it no more. She knew this and looked up at me and said,

"Don't you ever forget who's dick this is."

RESPECT REVENGE Pt. 1
"When Naptown Couldn't Sleep"

CHAPTER 32

The next day was Sunday and I usually went out to granny's crib to see her, but I needed to go visit someone else who was very near and dear to my heart. Plus, I needed to get my thoughts together and make sure I was seeing things for what they were and not for what they appeared to be. I made a stop at a flower shop, then headed to the cemetery to visit Keisha's grave.

    I pulled up, parked and got out. I walked across the grounds towards her resting place, and a feeling came over me that I couldn't describe. I had been in heated battles, where death whistled right past my head in the form of hot lead, but this here was the place you went when death had gotten his man. I arrived at her grave and brushed off her head stone. The reality off seeing her name, and years of Birth & Death weighed down on my chest heavily. I felt like I had killed her myself. See, that's why I didn't kill Falcon when I met him in the park that night. I had released the hounds myself, and in the process, brought death to my own flesh and blood. The person responsible for her death was Rico, not Falcon. When you're in the heat of battle, and someone

RESPECT REVENGE Pt. 1
"When Naptown Couldn't Sleep"

comes flying at you, you are in a kill or be killed situation. So I couldn't blame Falcon for reacting the same way, I would have. I learned something that night, something I was able to use to bring the war to a close. See when I first called Falcon that night, my intentions were to rock the nigga's block, but it would have been me acting off of pure emotions. Then when he said he had shot her eight times, I almost drew down and punished him. Then it hit me; if I almost acted off of emotion because of the loss of a loved one, then I could use the same shit against my opponent. So I killed Money's father, and sure enough, his failure to think had cost him his life. Big June had told me years before,

"If you can think, you can win. This is a thinking man's game."

Being at Keisha's grave, it helped me to come to terms with the situation a little better. So I sat down and talked to her spirit because her body was physically gone from our presence.

"Hey baby girl. I know you can hear me because angels return to heaven to look after the rest of us once they leave this hell that we call Earth. I know I could have and should have been there for you more, and for that I apologize. I never knew the nigga you were messing with was that nigga Rico, or I would have warned you about the caliber of dude you were messing with. I'm the one who gave the green light for Rico's life to be taken, so in all actuality, I sent your killers out there that night. I hope you can forgive me. I watch Granny and Auntie struggle to cope with your death all the time, and it kills me a little more every time I see it. I feel like if I could trade you places, and it be me who died, then I would, without hesitation. I l love you Keisha, and I'm sorry for the way things turned out. I pray that you have forgiven me. I'll be back to see you soon, I promise."

RESPECT REVENGE Pt. 1
"When Naptown Couldn't Sleep"

It was a rainy day and lightly sprinkling when I arrived, but as I headed back to my whip, the rain stopped and the sun started to shine. I stopped and looked back at her grave, and a rainbow was clearly visible across the sky. One single tear fell from my eye, because in my heart, I knew that me and baby were at peace.

RESPECT REVENGE Pt. 1
"When Naptown Couldn't Sleep"

CHAPTER 33

From there, I headed to Granny's crib out in Greenwood. Sunday dinner was just about to be served when I walked through the door. The first person to greet me was Baby Eric, who was 4 years old. He said,
"Momma! My Daddy here!"
I scooped my lil dude up and threw him up in the air a little bit, getting a good giggle out of him.
"How is Daddy's big man doin'?"
"I been good just like you told me, and I ain't let nobody mess wit my momma! I'm a big boy!"
"That's right, don't let nobody mess with your momma."
I put him down and told him to go and tell granny that I was here and to give her a hug for me. He took off like a bullet. That gave Sheen an opportunity to say what was on her mind.
"I'm finished with hair school and I'm tired of working at somebody else's shop. You told me that we would open up our own when I was ready. Well I'm ready. Plus, I'm ready for me and my son to move back into our own place."
 I looked at her and said, "Damn baby, can I answer one

RESPECT REVENGE Pt. 1
"When Naptown Couldn't Sleep"

question before you move on to the next one?"
"Go ahead then."
"Well, if you give me a month or two at the longest, I'll take care of the shop. Then soon after, I'll get ya'll settled in a new house." Then she said, "What about you? Are you coming back to live with yo family?" I knew that I didn't have a safe answer right then, so I said,
"We will talk about that when the time comes okay?"
We had been good together for a while, but she had turned a nigga off with her nagging ways. After I had started gettin' money and she saw twenty or thirty thousand, she started complaining about me being out all night and shit. She used to say shit like,
"You got money now, ain't no sense in you being out all times of the night."
She wanted me to lay around the house, and slow my roll and shit. But like I told her, that lil money was only the beginning, a nigga couldn't retire off of no money like that. Plus, everything we had came off of my blood, sweat, and tears. That drove a wedge between us and we haven't been right ever since. One thing was for sure though, I loved her and would never watch her struggle or want for nothing. She was there when a nigga didn't have shit, she helped me build this thang from the ground up. Just then granny walked in the room and bailed a nigga out.
"Hey son. How you been baby?"
"I'm good granny. I just left Keisha's grave site."
"Well, do you feel any better?
"Not really, because she gone, but I feel she is at peace with me. Granny said,
"Of course she is. That girl loved you to death. Come on in here and get you some of this food. Then I got a surprise for you."
Me, Granny, Sheen, and Baby Eric headed into the kitchen to eat, and I heard a toilet flush on the way down the hallway.

RESPECT REVENGE Pt. 1
"When Naptown Couldn't Sleep"

"Who that in the restroom Granny?"
"You will see, just sit down and eat."
I asked her, "Have you talked to Auntie Rhonda lately?"
"Yeah I talk to her every day. She told me to tell you to call her cause she miss hearing your voice and she worried about you."
 Auntie had been involved with this guy named Kenny, and they had gotten married and moved to Atlanta and opened up a couple of upscale clothing boutiques. She didn't want to stay here after losing Keisha, cause she said that she would never heal. As we were talking, I heard my father's voice coming out of the restroom.
"I know that ain't my sons voice I hear in there is it?"
At first, I looked at him with contempt, not because of anything he done to me. But because all he had put my granny through. But after seeing him and how good he was looking, I eased up and asked about his well-being.
 How you been old man?"
"I'm blessed, just got discharged two days ago. I been clean for six months and thirteen days as of today."
Granny had made me give her the money to send him to an inpatient drug treatment facility up-state. He had tried to quit smoking a thousand times, only to start back a thousand and one. So when she told me that for room and board, food, and six months' worth of programs, he needed $5,000 dollars, I thought of a million different ways that I could spend that kind of bread. But for granny, it was nothing.
 I said, "I'm glad you doin good. So what you gonna do out here in the free world?"
"I'm a stay out here with momma until I get me a job, then I'm a get my own place. I ain't goin' back to the hood."
I told Sheen to go get some money out of the bank and take him to get him some clothes. We couldn't have him walking around in

RESPECT REVENGE Pt. 1
"When Naptown Couldn't Sleep"

them tight ass pants. Everybody got a laugh out of that. We all sat there and enjoyed my granny's home cooking, and talked about this or that. I enjoyed being around my family, it was the only time that I could let my guard down and relax. After dinner, Granny and Sheen cleaned up the kitchen, and me and Baby Eric went to his room to play the video game. We played for about an hour and he just passed out right in the middle of the game. Granny peeked her head in just as I was putting the covers over little man. I walked out with her and she said,
"You know that boy loves you to death. You need to spend more time with him. Yeah, you spoil him, but ain't nothing like your time."
"I know Granny. I got to do better, these last 18 months have been hectic for me."
She said, "I know, come on in my room so we can talk."
Once we got in granny's room, she sat in her favorite chair and I laid across her bed, and she started right up.
    "You know you are my baby, I raised you and I know you better than you know yourself. I can see just by looking at you, that you had the weight of the world on your shoulders. But here recently, that storm has withered some. I watch the news, plus you know that I know everybody. I know a lot of what went on out there in them streets, even stuff that you didn't tell me. I don't judge much of what you do, but I feel like when you are in them streets on any level, you are subject to anything that comes with it. But when you work every day and are not involved in that foolishness, then it should never reach your door step. I don't know if you did it, or you just allowed it to be done, but whoever had a hand in the beating death of that older fella over on Tacoma, was dead wrong."
As she spoke, tears rolled down my face. I had never had any regrets about nobody I had murked, but I hated that I had done

RESPECT REVENGE Pt. 1
"When Naptown Couldn't Sleep"

pops Coleman the way I had. I had been at a loss on how to draw Money out in the open, and in war there is only one rule. And that is to win. Next, she brushed on the topic of Sheen.

"What are your plans for that girl? She been waiting and holding herself for you boy. She loves you to death and she feels like if she fool with anybody else, then that will be your excuse for not being with her. Then you don't make it no better because every time you come around, you take her up in that room and fornicate with her. You didn't think I knew that did you?" She smiled and continued, "Just make your mind up baby, either you want her or you don't. But stop leading her on. Let her go so she can have a life."

The shit my granny spit be so real, that a nigga feel like he been to church after listening to the jewels that she be dropping. She been around a while, and like she always says, "The only thing new under the sun, is the people on the Earth." In other words, the game don't change, just the players.

I hugged Granny and she prayed over me to be safe while I played on the devil's playground, as she called it. She told me to be careful and that she loved me, and I closed her door behind me.

I headed down to Sheen's room to say my good-byes. She was laying on her bed with a red thong on. Baby's body still looked like it did the first day I had met her. You couldn't even tell she had delivered a child. She was smelling all good and listening to R. Kelly's greatest hits. I eased in and closed the door behind me. She had her usual (Please come and fuck me before you go) face on. Granny had just told me about this, but how in the hell could I deny her something that was rightfully hers ...

RESPECT REVENGE Pt. 1
"When Naptown Couldn't Sleep"

CHAPTER
34

As I walked towards the bed, she rolled over onto her back and just watched me as I pulled my shirt over my head. She crawled up to the head of the bed and opened her night stand drawer and pulled out a freshly rolled blunt of that light green that she loved so much. I went and got in the shower that was connected to the master bedroom in which she stayed. After a quick shower, I was a lot more relaxed and with her standing there with a thick terry cloth bath towel to dry my body off, it made it all the more better.

    She handed me half of the blunt that she had saved me and lit it for me, then went about the business of drying me off. Once she finished, she grabbed my hand and led me to the bed where she had laid out towels and had her massage oils set up. She instructed me to lay on my stomach and rest my head on the pillow. She got on her knees beside me and began pouring scented oil all over me, then sat it down and started rubbing it in slowly. I closed my eyes and relaxed as she massaged my neck and back, then eased her way down, softly kissing and massaging straight down each leg all the way down to my feet.

RESPECT REVENGE Pt. 1
"When Naptown Couldn't Sleep"

By then, I was totally relaxed and she started giving attention to the head of my dick and balls that were peeking out from underneath me. She put her head between my legs and ran her tongue back and forth across them until she felt the dick getting hard. She told me to turn over and repeated a similar technique on the front side of my body. Once all of the caressing had taken place, she climbed on top of me and started sliding her body up and down mine. She was getting so aroused by this, and was staring me in the eyes the whole while. It seemed as if she got lost in the passion and started licking and kissing my neck and chest and didn't realize it until her face was between my legs. She caressed my private parts with her face, licking, kissing, and sucking me, seemingly turning herself on with her own actions. She looked up in between sucks and licks and said,

"My pussy is so wet right now and I need to feel you inside of me."

I was at a loss for words at that point. She started caressing my dick with her oily hands and then climbed on top and started riding me like she hadn't been fucked in a long time. Her excitement excited me and it felt like my dick was going to burst through the skin because it was so hard. She slowed down because she said that she didn't want me to cum yet, and she slowly pulled off of me so we could change positions. As she got up to do so, I felt like it was my turn to please so I grabbed her and turned her around and positioned her on the edge of the bed. I got even more turned on by seeing all that ass up in the air with that pretty pussy peeking out at me. I bent down and put my whole face in it and started licking her pussy and ass until she was damn near screaming out loud. After a nice taste of the main course, I grabbed the dick and slowly slid it in the pussy all the way to the balls, and baby let out a little whimper.

RESPECT REVENGE Pt. 1
"When Naptown Couldn't Sleep"

As I began to stroke it a lil bit, baby looked over her shoulder and hit me with a fuck face that told me that this is exactly what she had been missing. She came not even a full minute into it and not even a full minute after that, so did I.

She collapsed in a heap and lay there rubbing her legs together like a cricket would, with her eyes closed tightly. I watched her for a second and as I did, guilt came over me out of nowhere. The things granny had said to me not even 30 minutes ago came flooding into my consciousness. If I didn't want her, then why string her along? Was it that I couldn't stand the thought of her being with another man? Or did I want my cake and eat it too, simply because I could?

I went back in the bathroom and took a nice hot shower and allowed my thoughts to run wild with me. By the time I came out, the room was dark and baby appeared to be asleep. I didn't think she was really, but it was probably easier for her to hear me go than to see me and to have me further complicate things with another round of broken promises.

I stopped in to check on my son one more time before I left, then let myself out as I'd always done. I jumped in my whip and headed home to the one who I felt had my heart. About 10 minutes into my ride, my cell phone rung and it was Sheen calling. I looked at the caller I.D. and let the voice mail pick it up. I knew it was wrong not to answer, but if I did, I know it would only confuse things further than they already were. So I just turned my phone off completely. I would holla at her another time.

RESPECT REVENGE Pt. 1
"When Naptown Couldn't Sleep"

CHAPTER 35

Tuesday morning, I was up at the crack of dawn in anticipation on my call from Jake. I didn't know what to expect or how shit was gonna go, but I was ready to play ball. I had $160,000 rubber banned up in a duffle bag, and another $160,000 on standby. I had eaten breakfast and gave Ty some early morning dick, and sent her off to work. Now I was just sittin' here waiting on my phone to ring. Jake said that me and him were going to be the only one's using it, I didn't even know the number to the mufucka. About an hour later, it rang. I snatched it up immediately.
"Yeah?" It was Jake.
"What's up baby? You ready to roll?"
"Hell yeah. Just tell me where and when, and I'm there."
He said, "A'ight then, meet me at the Iron Skillet on West Washington St. in an hour. Come by yourself and leave your bread at home."
I didn't understand the leave my bread at home part, but he was the man, so I tucked the money under the bed and rolled out.
I arrived at the spot with 10 minutes' left to spare. It

RESPECT REVENGE Pt. 1
"When Naptown Couldn't Sleep"

was an upscale eatery, that served the business class, and people on their lunch break. Some were dressed casually, so I blended in with a royal blue, corduroy, Sean John outfit on.

As I looked around to see if I seen Jake, he flagged me down from a corner booth, where he was sitting by himself. He stood as I approached the table.

"What's good Big E?"

"What's up my dude?" And I took a seat across from him.

He said, "What are you driving?"

"The Black Tahoe right there."

"Give me your keys."

I didn't ask no questions, I just handed them over. A waitress came to our table,

"Welcome to the Iron Skillet, can I interest you in our specials today?" Jake told her no thanks and ordered a steak and eggs, with a black coffee. I ordered the same thang, but with an orange juice.

She said, "It will be about eight minutes; can I get you anything else?"

Jake told her no thanks, and she left. He went right to business.

"There is a blue F-150 parked on the side of the building with the keys in the ignition. The plates are legit and all the brake lights are in order. It is registered to a Mrs. Cassandra Sherrod. If you were to be pulled over, she would validate your story, claiming to be your Aunt. There is a space between the backseat and the truck bed that has been modified into a stash spot. The only way to access this spot is to put the truck in neutral, turn the windshield wipers on, hold your foot on the brake, and push in the cigarette lighter. With that a latch will release and the back seat will be able to fold down, revealing the stash spot. We already discussed the ticket for each brick, so you'll know what you owe me once you see what's inside. When you get done, take

RESPECT REVENGE Pt. 1
"When Naptown Couldn't Sleep"

the money and put it in the compartment and then you call me and tell me where to meet you for lunch. That is how we handle business.

This nigga Jake had his shit together. This car sounded like some shit straight out of a James Bond flick. I guess when you gettin' it like he gettin' it, then you got to be on some official shit. Once our food arrived and we finished eating, he dropped a C-note on the table and told me that someone would bring my Tahoe to me later on. Then he said,
 "When you set up the lunch dates, the bill is on you."
I asked him, "So how does the F-150 ride?"
He looked at me and smiled, then said,
"I don't know, I ain't never been in the muthafucka." And he walked out.

RESPECT REVENGE Pt. 1
"When Naptown Couldn't Sleep"

CHAPTER
36

I left there and headed straight to Ty's house. I pulled the truck into the garage and made the truck do its magic trick. When I folded down the seat, I almost passed out. Once I had pulled out the bricks and counted them out, I had four piles of ten. This nigga had just fronted me 40 kilos'.

I put the work back in the stash spot. Where better to keep them, than a place where they couldn't be found. I had an apartment that I had rented in a white neighborhood that I had planned to keep the work, but for now, I would just play it like this. Now it was time to do the math and figure out the break down with this shit.

First of all, I had to feed my team. I had Harvey, who was getting five bricks to sell in the hood. He would handle all of the sells from an 8-ball to an ounce. He would give me a total of $26,000 per brick. So off of him alone, I would make $130,000 for the five birds. His take would be a free $30,000. He never had to worry about being robbed because we were the robbers, plus we had security in the hood, so the streets were protected.

Then I had B-Boy and Lil Kev. They had their

RESPECT REVENGE Pt. 1
"When Naptown Couldn't Sleep"

individual blocks jumpin' 24/7. They had workers curb serving for them around the clock. They had all the fiends in the hood sowed up. I'd give them a brick a piece to hold their blocks down. They had to give me $26,000 as well because I owned them blocks and they had to pay due's. They were making way more than Harvey because they were bustin' the work down, and gettin' every dime. So that's another $52,000.

    Then, I had Lucky and Cookie Face. They would get five bricks apiece, for the same price I was payin' for them. Them niggas had helped take over these streets, and they deserved to eat. Plus, I knew that they were real and loyal niggas, and you don't find them like that too often. So out of 40 of them thangs, 17 were already spoken for, and that left me with 23 to do me with. I was going to take em' to the streets and let em' fly for $22,000 apiece. So my profit off of the 23 would be $138,000. So when you added it all up, off of the entire 40, I would pull in $848,000, of which I owed Jake $640,000. So my total profit per flip would be $208,000.

    That was good muthafuckin' money considering the fact that I hadn't put up a single dollar. I'm a push my squad to flip this shit twice a month in the beginning, then try to make it twice a fuckin' week if I can.

    Later that same day, I met with Harvey, and dropped him off his issue and told him let's work. Fam' got right down to business. Next I hit B-Boy and Lil Kev, and told them the plans for their block's, they was wit it 100%. Then I had Cookie and Lil Lucky meet me at one of our spots in the hood. They came immediately, wondering why I was sounding so anxious. When I handed them nigga's that duffle bag with the ten brick's inside and told them to split that, and then only give me $16,000. per loaf. Them nigga's damn near died. They knew they was about to see money like they had never seen it before. I told them I had to

RESPECT REVENGE Pt. 1
"When Naptown Couldn't Sleep"

go because I had to holla at them cat's that I had been hollering at that night at the Mecca. The one's I had told what my new price's was gonna be. They had talked that big money shit, but now that I had them in my possession, it was time to show and prove. Cookie took their dope and went to go stash it. Lucky went with me for security.

I called this nigga from Clifton St. named Frank. He wanted three of em' off the rip. Then I got with another cat from over there named Cake's, he ordered up two for himself and two for his partner. When the dope is good, plus the price is $3,000 better than the rest of the competition, money starts coming out of the woodworks. I looked up and 10 days later, I didn't have a crumb of dope left. I was just waiting on the rest of the team to come through with theirs.

The next day, Lucky and Cookie were finished with theirs. They did the smart thing. They secured me for the whole ten days that it took me to fleece mine's, then once I ran out, they served the same people that were waiting for me to re-up. Harvey called my phone and told me he was finished, he had served five brick's worth of quarters, half's, and ounce's. I was impressed. I knew that B-Boy and Kev would take a lil longer than everybody else, because they were small doggin' theirs trying to bleed them blocks dry. So I wasn't going to let the $52,000 they owed me, stop me from gettin' back at Jake.

So, 12 days after I received that first call from Jake, I placed a call of my own. He answered on the third ring. "Talk to me Big E!"

I said, "I ain't doin' shit, just chillin', kind of hungry. I'm getting ready to go over to the Country Kitchen on College Ave. and get me some of that soul food everybody be talking bout."

RESPECT REVENGE Pt. 1
"When Naptown Couldn't Sleep"

He said, "Aw yeah. Well I could use a bite to eat myself. I guess I'll see you in an hour then." Then he hung up.

I loaded up the truck with the $640,000 that I owed him and headed towards College Ave ...

RESPECT REVENGE Pt. 1
"When Naptown Couldn't Sleep"

CHAPTER 37

When I walked in the Country Kitchen, Jake was sitting at a table by the wall in the back reading the paper. He looked up and saw me and gave me an approving smile.
　"What's up my guy?"
I answered, "What's happening with you?"
"I'm good, just surprised to be having lunch with you so soon. It ain't been nothing but 12 days. You gettin' down like that?"
I told him, "Yeah, I'm out there, plus the West ain't saw no numbers like that in a long time. They goin' crazy out there."
"So, how are they treating the new weather man on the Westside?"
"You know, same as always. I gets love and I gets hate. With these numbers, I'm steppin on a lot of toe's. Everything good right now, but it's way too early to tell. But if any problems arise, I'm a handle it swiftly. You can believe that."
　Jake spoke up, "Let me give you a lil piece of advice. Money and murder don't mix. So if you can avoid drama, then do so, for the sake of us gettin' this money. But if you got to send a message or set an example to show them streets that you mean business, do so by all means, just don't make

RESPECT REVENGE Pt. 1
"When Naptown Couldn't Sleep"

no habit of it. When them bodies get to droppin', you will get the attention of them alphabet boy's, and that's not healthy, you feel me? I know you and your squad came up from the dirt, but shit done changed for ya'll now. It's time for ya'll to get this paper. Get some of them young soldiers and make em' earn their way like you did. You on another level now."

    I could feel the game that this nigga was droppin' in my lap. I knew that in order for me to have a good run in this game, I would have to respect the rule's. Jake told me that I would hear from him in the next 24 hours on where I could pick up the truck with the next 40 bricks. I dapped him up and rolled out. I had 24 hours to burn, I figured I would go spend a lil time with my baby momma ...

Over the next three months, me and Jake played phone tag a couple of times a month. Shit was runnin' smooth. The drop off's and pick up's remained the same.

The money on the Westside was flowing and you could just look and tell, everybody was shining. I had so much money laying around that it caught the attention of Ty.

    "Baby, what are you gonna do with all this money? I got a couple of ideas on how to clean it up." She ran her plans by me and it made plenty of sense. She quit the real estate firm that she had been working at for the last three years, and leased some office space and opened up her own. We was 50/50 partners, with my half going in my Auntie Rhonda's name. Once she got that up and running, I was our best customer. We started buying up all the abandoned houses in my hood, as well as two apartment buildings. Then she opened up a home renovation and repair business in my father's name and hired him to run it. Next she bought a beauty shop on the Westside, and remodeled it and named it the New Doo. Me and Sheen owned that. My father had hired experienced workers at our home renovation

RESPECT REVENGE Pt. 1
"When Naptown Couldn't Sleep"

business, and they were working on all the houses we had bought in the hood. But most importantly, this money now had some foundation. We were cleaning it up and giving Uncle Sam his proper chop. It was November of "1999" and the new millennium was fast approaching. Now that everything was leveling out and running smoothly, I had plans for me and my inner circle to bring the new year in like the big boys do ...

RESPECT REVENGE Pt. 1
"When Naptown Couldn't Sleep"

CHAPTER 38
New Year's Eve 2,000!

Me, Ty, Lil Lucky, and Cookie had flown down to Miami for the new year. My nigga Jake had given me and my family the invite. We were staying in this beachfront property, overlooking the ocean. There were yachts and boats all over the place. Muthafucka's were on jet skis and bitch's were walking around in bikini's, and it was December.

    Later that night, we were getting ready to go to the New Year's party out on a 262-foot yacht. I had on an all-white, custom fitted Armani suit, with some ostrich skin, soft bottom shoe's that had hit me for a pretty penny. I was wearing a platinum, presidential Rolex, with the pinky ring to match. My cuff links were the initials of my hood. One was a diamond studded H, the other was a P. The Hard-Part was definitely in the building. I had went to the shop and let Sheen whip my hair in some exotic design that she had came up with so yo boy was on point. I looked like a million bucks and felt like I was worth even more.

    At 11:00 sharp, a stretch Hummer pulled up at the spot and we all climbed in and were driven to the yacht. We got out of the Hummer and were amazed. This ship looked

RESPECT REVENGE Pt. 1
"When Naptown Couldn't Sleep"

like a space ship out on the water. It was the middle of the night and this mufucka was lit up like a Christmas tree. You could see people on all three levels of the ship were in full party mode. Me and my squad had never really been out of the city, and we were like kids in a candy store for the first time. We headed up the ramp and my nigga Lucky was like,
 "Man, this shit here is on some Noriega, Pablo Escobar type shit!" We all started laughing, and I said,
"Yeah, but the Hard-Part is on deck!"
Once we got on board, we were escorted to a ballroom on the second floor, where we were met by Jake, who took us to a big ass table where his man Juan-C and some cat that I assumed was Juan-C's partner were seated. Also at the table were three bad ass Dominican bitch's. Jake made introductions all around and then said,
    "What's good E baby?" "How was the flight?"
"Everything was all good, but this boat is a bad mufucka!"
Jake said, "A boat is what you fish on, this here is some shit I could live on!"
The nigga Juan-C rose to give a nigga some dap, but he had this sour ass look on his face all of a sudden. This was the second time this nigga's mood had struck me as odd. I don't know why, but I definitely wasn't feelin' this cat. But fuck this nigga, he probably hating cause he ain't the only one gettin' them thangs at a discount rate in the city. I came to Miami to enjoy the fruits of my labor, and I wasn't going to let this nigga, and his hate fuck up my mood.
    It turned out that the owner of the yacht was this Dominican drug lord named Raul. He had at least one major player from each of the major cities pushing weight for him, all were in attendance. Most of them even had bought a few of their best men, and we were living it up on this eve of a new

RESPECT REVENGE Pt. 1
"When Naptown Couldn't Sleep"

millennium. There were ice sculptures and champagne fountains, plus the biggest buffet of fresh fruit and slice meats that I'd ever seen. The music was of a mixed variety, but to my surprise, mostly hip hop. Most of the rnuthafucka's in here were black, I guess if you need your dope pushed in the ghettos of America, then you get a black mufucka to do it. Me and Ty got up to dance after a few drinks. Jake told the rest of the crew," make sure ya'll mingle because all of these Dominican hoe's in here are single!"

Lucky and Cookie were definitely feelin' that. They disappeared into the crowd, R. Kelly's song, "Seem's like you're ready" came on and me and Ty got close for a slow dance. She said, "What's wrong with that dark skinned guy Juan-C, or whoever he is? He was enjoying himself and having a good time as we approached the table, but when he saw us, his whole demeanor changed."

I said, "I peeped him, but I ain't gonna let no hate fuck up our first vacation. Plus, I'm holding the flyest lady in the room, and I got my mind on gettin' some tonight."
"Boy stop, I'm in here trying to get chose tonight."
"Girl, don't get nobody killed in this muthafucka!"
She said, "Naw, I'm just playin'. I'm glad to be with the realest nigga in the room, and I'm a ride with you until you don't want me no more, then I'm a stalk you."

Just as we were talking, a dark brown skinned man, with a long, curly ponytail walked up on the stage and grabbed the microphone. He had two of the biggest mufucka's I had ever seen standing on either side of him. The Dominican spoke into the mic in very broken English. "Good evening my friends. Tonight marks the beginning of a brand new beginning, this is the eve of a new millennium. We will continue to live the American dream, deep into the future, enjoy yourselves and have the time of your life, everything is on me!" We headed back to the table, where

RESPECT REVENGE Pt. 1
"When Naptown Couldn't Sleep"

everyone had met back up and grabbed bottles of bubbly, and the countdown began 10,9,8, 7, I looked my squad in their eyes, and I knew that they knew what I was thinking. It was us against the world. 4,3,2,1,"Happy New Year!" The crowd went crazy. We partied hard deep into the night, and off into the morning, then Me and Ty jumped into the stretch Hummer and went back to the place we were staying. Cookie and Lucky hung back with Jake and his men on the yacht with some of them Dominican mommies and brought their new year in the same way I did, freakin' wit something sexy.

    Jake came through the next morning and scooped me up in a big body Benz. Me, him and Juan-C rode to a gated community and rode up a driveway that seemed to be a mile long. The house was some shit straight off of the lifestyles of the rich and famous.

    I knew off the muscle that this was some major shit. We were escorted to a library, where the same short Dominican that spoke on the yacht last night, was seated behind a desk with the same two body guards on standby. One was right behind him, the other was by the door. The man said,

    "Hey Jake, How you doin'?"
"I'm good Raul, just stoppin' through before me and my family leave town."
Raul said, "Did you enjoy yourself at the party?"
"We did, and it was something that I'm sure none of us will never forget."
"I see that you have a new member of your family with you."
"Yeah, this is Big E, he is a strong member of my team. He has proven himself in both war and worth. I trust him like I trust myself."
Raul said, "Is that so? How are you doin' big E?" I spoke up.
 "I'm good sir. How are you?"

RESPECT REVENGE Pt. 1
"When Naptown Couldn't Sleep"

"Sir is not necessary. You are a part of my extended family now, if Jake trusts you, then so do I. I must extend the same welcome to you, that I extend to all of my family members. If you ever need to get out of the city, or just need a vacation, I have 10 beach front properties here in Miami. You are more than welcome."

"I appreciate that."

He said, "No I appreciate you. People think what I do is easy. That's because it's made to look easy because the people I employ are good at what they do. Jake has been with me many years; he is a good judge of character. He has been successful, and I'm sure you will be too. Just remember this. Loyalty is a trait of honor. Honor is a trait of respect. They are all the traits of a real man. Always deal with a man, like a man."

Me, Jake and Juan-C left the mansion and I had a feeling that those were more than just words. They were a welcome, as well as a warning ...

RESPECT REVENGE Pt. 1
"When Naptown Couldn't Sleep"

CHAPTER
39

We got back into town and everything was all good. Me, Lucky and Cookie kept the clamps on the Westside. I had just copped a cocaine white, 2000, 600 Benz. I put it on some 20" inch Lexani's. I had them haters foaming at the mouth, and the nigga's who respected the game, wanting to get they grind on. A few months had gone by since I had met Raul. Jake had told him how I got down with my gun game, so when he had some problems in Cincinnati that he needed solved, he asked if I could handle it.

Raul's man in Cincinnati had been kidnapped and tortured, and ultimately taken for $1.5 million cash, and fifty kilos of coke.

The nigga's name was Lil Zach. Zach had been found dead in the trunk of his car with his throat cut and burns all over his body. His security people had went into hiding because none of them knew the connect and now that Zach was dead they were like fuck him. His right hand man had flown down to Miami and gave Raul the run-down on the whole situation. He said he was willing to step up and fill the shoes of Lil Zach, but he wasn't a killer and didn't have the

RESPECT REVENGE Pt. 1
"When Naptown Couldn't Sleep"

means in which to deal with the problem. So Raul sent the nigga back to Cincinnati and told him his people would be there soon. Me, Lil Lucky and Cookie were his people.
We got to Cincinnati a couple days after I got the call. The right hand man, whose name was Black Darryl met us at the airport in a 2000 Suburban, all black with the tinted windows. He rode us around showing us where the dudes responsible be at.

They had a building on a half of a block that had a pool hall, a variety store, and a beauty shop, all connected together. This was a high traffic area that I could tell was a lot like my very own corner, an open air drug market. Where there's drugs, there were niggas', where there were nigga's, there were gun's. This was not going to be no one day job.

The two dudes responsible were two brothers named Damon and Raymon. They ran a clique of nigga's that were known for a little bit of everything from hustlin', to robbery, extortion and even murder.

The nigga Black Darryl was evidently shook by these nigga's, he didn't even like riding through the area. He took us to a crib where we would stay until we got our man. He pulled a suit case out from under a bed and opened it up and showed us a nice lil arsenal of weapons. He had Mack 1O's, Mack 11's, twin .45's, 357's, and a sawed off shotgun. We got settled in and he gave us the keys to the crib and the suburban and then left. We strapped up with a few handguns and decided to go play a little pool.

Once we got to the pool hall, I realized why Raul elected to send niggas instead of his Dominican hitters. These nigga's was on point. They was watching us like hawks, and we looked just like them. Them Dominicans would have stuck out like sore thumbs. I had a plan and had already ran it by my nigga's. We were going to come here every day until somebody asked us who we were, then I would say we were from Dayton Ohio and we

RESPECT REVENGE Pt. 1
"When Naptown Couldn't Sleep"

was trying to holler at Damon and Raymon about a lil business, because it was a drought in our city. I figured if I played to these nigga's greed, I might get somewhere. They had fifty bricks laying around, and I knew they would be trying to dump em' off.

Nobody said nothing the first day, so we switched up our style on day number two. I got dressed in a Gucci, blue jean outfit, with some gum sole Gucci boots to match. I wore a simple Gucci link chain, with a Jesus piece that hung down to my navel. Cookie and Lucky played the role of security, standing by watching my back while I played pool and offered to beat anybody willing. Looking like money changed everything. We hadn't been in the spot 30 minutes, when a tall lanky nigga eased up on the table and said,

"What's your name homie?" I acted like I didn't hear him at first, then answered,

"They call me J-Moe. Why what's up?"

"I just asked because I saw you and your mans' an em' round here yesterday, and it don't be too many new faces round here."

"Well, I'm just lookin for Damon or Raymon. You know either one of them?"

"Yeah I know em'. Let me get my man T-Loc for you."

T-Loc was another skinny nigga but he looked like he meant business. He walked over to the table and said,

"What's up partner? What you want wit my peoples?"

I told him, "I'm up here from Dayton and I'm trying to see your people's bout a lil bidness before I head out. I'm only going to be here a couple more days before I bounce."

He said, "Where you staying at?"

"I'm stayin' at the other end of this number." I gave him my cell number.

"Tell yo peoples to get at me if possible and I'll swing back through."

RESPECT REVENGE Pt. 1
"When Naptown Couldn't Sleep"

After that I signaled Cookie and Lucky, and we was out.
The trap was set, so all I had to do was see if the old saying was true. Greed will cost you more than you will gain.
The next day around 1:00, we were chillin' at the spot watching some old Mike Tyson fights on H.B.O., when my prepaid cell phone rang. I picked it up,
    "Yeah, who dis?"
    "This Damon, what's up?"
"This J-Moe, the nigga that was at your spot yesterday, I been trying to see you."
"How you been trying to see me and you don't even know me?"
"Your name is ringin' all the way down in Dayton, and I hear you the man to see round here."
He said, "enough said on this phone, swing through the pool hall, I'll be there in an hour."
Then he hung up. We locked and loaded and mounted up.
When we got to the pool hall, it was loaded down with nigga's faking like they was playing pool. I guess they were there to make sure that everything was everything. When I walked through the door I was told that Damon was waiting for me in the back office. I started to walk back there and was told that I couldn't take no gun back there. I pulled the .357 snub nose out of my waist and handed it to Cookie, and they played pool while I went to holla. Damon was a short brown skinned muscular dude, with jail house tattoo's all over his arms, and two tear drops under his eye. He looked me up and down, and said,
    "What's up cuz?"
I laid my bull-shit story about being from Dayton, and it being a drought on work down there. Then he said,
"So what made you come to my place of business looking for some work?"
 I was two steps ahead of him. I had asked the nigga Black Darryl

RESPECT REVENGE Pt. 1
"When Naptown Couldn't Sleep"

for the name of any hustler whose name I could drop that would put this nigga at ease, just in case the situation ever arose. He had given me one, so I said,
     "I use to come down and deal with Baby Tony and them nigga's up town, but they stopped being able to handle my order, and one of em' mentioned your name to me." He fell right in, "Aw yeah? Them broke ass nigga's up town been getting their work from us."
When he said that, I knew I had him. Then he asked me, "So what you trying to get?"
"I'll take 4 or 5 of them thangs if you can handle it."
"Come on now, you wouldn't have came sniffin' around here if you didn't think I could handle it. You already know that I be hittin' for $28,000 a slab right?"
This nigga was trippin'. If I had been trying to get right for real, I would have been seriously offended at a price so high, but under the circumstances, I agreed like the nigga was showing me some love.
 "A'ight, how soon can you have me together?"
He said, "How soon can you have that bread?"
 "I can be back here within the hour."
As I was leaving, he picked up the phone and spoke into it, "Put Raymon on the phone ...Who the fuck you think it is! It's Damon!"
I knew then that they both would probably be here when we came back. Then I could kill two birds with one stone ...

RESPECT REVENGE Pt. 1
"When Naptown Couldn't Sleep"

CHAPTER
40

I figured they would have a few Goon's and guns hanging around when we came back, but I had a plan to clear the spot out and give us a minute or two to be about our business. We sat around a table and went over the plan. I had to use the nigga Black Darryl, our so called guide if this shit was going to work.

Me and my guys strapped up with Mack 1O's and jumped in the Suburban and parked down the street from the pool hall. Darryl was at the other end of the block in a mini-van facing our direction. Just as I had thought, there was three dudes hanging outside of the pool hall, I knew there were at least four more inside. The tall lanky doorman, the security nigga T-Loc, and hopefully the two nigga's that I came to see. I picked up my cell phone and dialed Black Darryl's number. He answered immediately.

"Yeah?"

I asked him, "You ready?"

"Yeah I'm ready."

"Then go ahead and do your thang."

The mini-van pulled up in front of the pool hall and Darryl

RESPECT REVENGE Pt. 1
"When Naptown Couldn't Sleep"

rolled his window down and aimed a pistol at the crowd and said, "I'll lay all you bitch's down right now! Say something!"
They knew that he was one of Lil Zach's boys and he was faking, so they jumped in an old L.T.D. that was parked at the curb and gave chase. As soon as Cookie saw that the plan had worked, he pulled the Suburban right in front of the pool hall and we stormed the door on foot. By the time the door man saw the hardware, he froze up. I grabbed him by the neck.
"Cooperate and you live! Get buck and you get killed!"
Lucky held down the door, just in case the L.T.D. came back, and Cookie rushed towards the office door with his Mack trained on it. I pushed the doorman towards the office and told him,
 "Do whatever you would do if we came on business." He understood.

He knocked and said, "T-Loc, dude and em' out here!" The door came open and the nigga T-Loc was coming out. Cookie hit the nigga in the mouth with the butt of the Mack, causing him to stumble back into the office. The dude Damon had been on the phone with his feet kicked up, the other stud, who I assumed was Raymon, was sitting in a chair against the wall. He went to reach in his waist for his burner and I hit that nigga with 3 quick ones' in his chest with the Mack. I shoved the doorman into T-Loc, while Cookie had his weapon trained on Damon. I told the doorman and
T-Loc to lay face down. T-Loc had a look of defiance on his face, so I showed him that I wasn't playin. I hit him in the thigh with a hot one, and that helped him to the floor with the quickness. He was rolling around holding his leg in terrible pain. Cookie switched and covered them while I dealt with Damon.

I said, "Man, you know what this is don't you?"
"Man, you can have the dope! Take it, it's in the bag!"
"Man fuck that dope! This about Lil Zach and your disrespect for

RESPECT REVENGE Pt. 1
"When Naptown Couldn't Sleep"

the man that I work for!"
He started to say something, and I hit him in the face with two quick, one's.
"Boc! Boc!"
Rap was dead. Literally. Cookie opened fire on T-Loc, taking him out of his misery. The tall, lanky doorman was layin' on the floor shaking like he was having a seizure.
"Please don' t kill me! I got kids!"
I said, "Man, fuck your kids! Stand up!"
I walked right up in his face and said,
"I'm a let you live cause I need someone to pass on this message for me. The next time my peoples send some dope to Cincinnati, if ya'll can't afford to buy it, then you better leave it alone! If ya'll don't, then we will make the murder rate in this mufucka go way up, believe that! Now lay down on you face and count to 100!"

Cookie grabbed the bag that held the five brick's, and we was out. Lucky seen us comin', and jumped in the Suburban and we smashed. As we were pulling off, the L.T.D. was pulling up to the curb. They were in for the surprise of their lives.

I called Black Darryl and asked him was he straight. He was cool and was waiting for us at the spot. We pulled up 5 minutes later and he was sweating bullets. Soon as we hit the door, he started asking stupid ass questions,
"Did ya'll get em'? Ya'll think they gonna know that I had something to do with it?"
"Be easy man, everything gonna be straight."
I had sent Lucky around to the gas station to get some gas. Cookie was gettin' our few little things together, cause we was getting ready to make the three hour ride back to Nap-Town in our borrowed Suburban.

Ten minutes later, Lucky walked in the door with a red gas can in his hand. I got up and grabbed our things and headed

RESPECT REVENGE Pt. 1
"When Naptown Couldn't Sleep"

to the truck. By the time I got the truck loaded and went back into the crib, I think the cat knew he was in a fucked up situation. He had this real nervous look on his face.
He said, "Hey man, am I straight?"
I told him, "Yeah, you good, calm down. But listen, if you was Lil Zach's right hand man, then he never stood a chance in the first place."
Lucky eased up behind him and put one behind his ear with a .38, he was dead before he hit the floor.
See, Raul had no respect for this faggot. Your man gets tortured and killed and your first move was to jump on a plane and try to take his place? There was no honor or respect in that. Raul had told me to send a message to Cincinnati, and make sure to leave someone alive to spread the word, but make sure it wasn't this coward. Again, he spoke his previous words.
"Deal with men, like men. But don't deal with cowards at all."
Once me and Lucky made it to the truck, Cookie doused the place with gas, and sent any traces of Darryl or us ever being there, up in smoke. We jumped in the truck and headed back to the Hard-Part ...

RESPECT REVENGE Pt. 1
"When Naptown Couldn't Sleep"

CHAPTER
41

When I got back, everything was still in order. Harvey had held shit down while we were gone. The only news was that the nigga Lil Dave had gotten out and wanted to see me. Lil Dave use to be Big June's right hand man when I first started out on the corner. He is the one who had given me the pistol to rob Taco when I was a shorty. He had caught a case and went and done a lil bid. Now he was out. I was curious to see where his head was at because when he left, we wasn't really on nothing. Now, we ran the whole Westside. I hoped he would just fall in line and play his position, we would soon see.

    It was a Sunday afternoon in June of 2000, and the Westside was out in droves. Everybody and their momma was at Riverside Park flossin' they best whips and gettin' they shine on. It was so many hoe's out there it wasn't even funny. The park is like that every Sunday of the summer. They had barbeque's goin' everywhere, the ballers were doin' they thang on the court, it was all love. But if I knew the Westside like I thought I did, someone would be shooting as soon as, or not long after it got dark. Me, Cookie and Lil Lucky had

RESPECT REVENGE Pt. 1
"When Naptown Couldn't Sleep"

brought our bike's out this day. We had bought these joints with some of the proceeds from the work we put in for Raul. He had sent me a blessing for providing my services, and I split it three ways.
We were in the shade gettin' at some lil hood rats, when the nigga Lil Dave walks up.
  "Lil E, what's good baby? I been lookin' for you. I see you shinin' out here. You lookin good."
"What's up Lil Dave? When they free you?"
"I been out a couple of weeks now. I had just missed you before you left town."
I said, "Yeah, so what up wit you?"
"Man, you already know I'm finna' get me out here. You gonna hit my hand or what?"
"You know I got you, just fall back and peep shit out and figure out what you want to do and get with me when you ready. But hold on to this for now."
I went in my pocket and gave him the $2,500 that I had on me. He said, "Good lookin' Lil Homie, I'm a be at you, you hear me?"
"Yeah I hear you, but that Lil Homie shit ain't gonna fly."
 "Damn my nigga, I ain't mean nothing by it. I just remember you bein' a little dude when I ran the corner, that's all."
I stuck my fist out and clapped the nigga up, and he rolled out. I knew Lil Lucky was going to say something immediately.
  "I don' t like that nigga, nor do I trust him."
 I said, "Damn Lil Lucky, the nigga ain't even done nothing."
"That's the point! The nigga ain't done nothing. Coming round here like a nigga owe him something. He rubbed me the wrong way wit that Lil Homie shit."
I said, "He wasn't even talkin' to you, he said it to me."
 "I know he didn't say it to me, cause I probably would have

RESPECT REVENGE Pt. 1
"When Naptown Couldn't Sleep"

clapped his ass right there where he stood!"
    Me and Cookie bust out laughing. Lucky's little man complex had surfaced once again.
The next time I saw Lil Dave was a month later. He was with this nigga from the hood named Rude. They were on Burton Ave. on Ms. Jones's porch when I came through. I walked up on the porch and showed them both some love.
    "What's up my nigga's?"
Lil Dave said, "What's happening "E". We ain't doing shit, just sittin' back gettin' our lungs dirty. You trying to hit this shit?"
I grabbed the blunt and took a hit of the stress, I ain't want to be rude, then went in my pocket and pulled out a quarter ounce of that "Joe Jackson". That shit that will beat your lungs up and make em' sing out after every pull. I gave the sack to Rude, and he twisted one up while I hollered at Lil Dave. Me and Lil Dave walked off of the porch, and out of ear shot of Rude. I asked him,
"Have you figured out your angle yet? What you trying to do?"
"Yeah, you know that I know the whole Westside, I can really move some weight out here. Just hit my hand and I'm a show you how I get this money."
    I told him, "Well this is what I'm a do. I'm a drop a couple of them thangs on your lap, make it do what it do, then we will go from there. I'm not going to tell you how to sell it, cause you are a straight up hustler and I know it. You can hit the blocks, serve it in weight, or do both. I'm giving you the green light to do what you do in the hood.
    I fronted Lil Dave two bricks for $22,000 apiece. He flipped them in four days. He hit me with my bread, plus some of his own, so I threw him four of em' to hold him off. The nigga was fleecin' the work like it was going out of style. He made Harvey mad because he never slept and Harvey use to

RESPECT REVENGE Pt. 1
"When Naptown Couldn't Sleep"

have people waiting on him all day long. Now if he took too long, they would hit up Lil Dave. He flipped and flopped the work for the next six months, passing up Harvey quickly, so I decided to put the nigga on for real. I dealt with him, and he dealt with everybody else.
I fell back, and so did Lucky and Cookie. We had impressed Raul with our efficiency so much that, any time he had a problem in the Midwest, instead of sending his black-out teams all the way from Miami, he just called me. We had been to Columbus Ohio, Cleveland, Detroit, Chicago twice, and St. Louis since our lil trip to Cincinnati. After them jobs, we were financially straight. I had been spending time with Tyesha, just traveling around the country. We were packing up getting ready to head out to Vegas for a week, when my business phone rang.
"Yeah, what's up?"
Jake asked, "Can you and your squad get together and be ready to go to Louisville?"
"You know me, I can have me and mine's ready to roll in a couple of hours."
"Good, I'm sending Juan-C with you. He knows everything and everybody down there, he will point you in the right direction."
I didn't like dealing with this nigga, but I couldn't let my personal feelings get in the way of business. So I agreed and told Jake that I would be out east in a couple of hours.

    I hit Lil Lucky and Cookie and told them that we had work to do and to get ready to roll out. Before I left, I met with Lil Dave and gave him the 15 bricks that I had left. For the last 8 or 9 months he had been runnin' through them thangs like candy. I usually gave them to him as needed, but I had no idea when I would be back, so I might as well make sure he had enough to hold him over. Once I got the business straight, I scooped up my squad, and we headed to the east side ...

RESPECT REVENGE Pt. 1
"When Naptown Couldn't Sleep"

CHAPTER
42

We met up over one of Juan-C's cribs in Brightwood. This was the same hood where my lil cousin Keisha had got killed, so she crossed my mind as we pulled up in the nigga's drive way. We were pushing the F-150 with the stash spot and a Cadillac S.T.S. Me and Juan-C hopped in the S.T.S and Cookie, Lucky and Juan-C's man loaded the guns into the stash spot in the truck, jumped in, and we hit the highway headed towards Louisville.

We were about halfway there, when we were pulled over for speeding by a state trooper.
"Whoop! Whoop!" We Pulled over to the shoulder and the cop tapped on the window with his flashlight.
"Can I see some license, registration, and proof of insurance please?"
"Yeah, here you go."
Juan-C handed him the documents through the window. The cop looked them over, then looked at Juan C and said,
"Dejuan Coleman is it? Where are you in such a rush to get to Mr. Coleman?"
"I didn't realize that I was speeding officer, but I'm headed

RESPECT REVENGE Pt. 1
"When Naptown Couldn't Sleep"

down to Louisville to a car show."
    "Have you had anything to drink tonight Mr. Coleman?"
"No sir."
"Is there anything in this car that I should know about? Guns, Knives or drugs?"
"No sir."
"Okay, hold tight here, while I run your name for warrants."
He went back to his squad car to run his check. Right then, my instincts told me something was wrong, but I chalked it up to being pulled over, while on the way to kill for money. He let us off with a warning, and we went on about our business. I made the call to the fella's in the truck to tell them we were straight.

    We got to Louisville about an hour later, and went to this apartment complex on Utah Ave. These were Louisville's version of projects. This job wasn't from Raul, some nigga from our own city named Muncie had run off with 20 bricks that belonged to Jake. But Jake had only fucked with the nigga on the strength of Juan-C. So he was making Juan-C take part in either gettin em' back or killin' the cat. He sent us down to make sure shit went right and the problem was solved.

    The nigga Juan-C knew the dude Muncie had set up shop right here in this same apartment complex, so he had came down and rented us a couple of units for us to chill in, while we laid on this nigga. We watched out of windows for a week straight, as these nigga's made a killin' serving hand to hand, right out in the open. The police would whip up, jump out, and take niggas to jail damn near every day. Every time a Ford Taurus or a van bent the block, they knew what time it was.

    What finally caught my attention was a black, 2-door, Lexus Coup that would pull in to the parking lot every day and wait on this tall light skinned cat with dreads to come out of his apartment and jump in the car with him. We couldn't see

RESPECT REVENGE Pt. 1
"When Naptown Couldn't Sleep"

who was in the car because the Coup had tinted windows, but I figured that it might be our man in there. But whoever it was, we couldn't be sure because he never got out. We needed to know, so Lil Lucky volunteered to check it out.

The next day when the Coup pulled up, Lucky eased out of the apartment as soon as the tall nigga with the dreads got into the car. Everyone knows that if you get close enough to a car, you could see through the windshield because the windshields aren't tinted, just the top strip. So lucky figured he would walk right up to the car and look. Either way, rather it was or it wasn't him, he would just keep walking. When Lucky got up to the car bumper, the driver door flew open and true enough it was him. He hopped out of the car and charged Lucky with a .44 Bull-dog in his hand. Before anyone could react, he hit lucky in the face with 2 rounds from the murder weapon. **"Boom! Boom!"**

"What Ya'll think I'm stupid! I knew they would send somebody after me!"
Then he stood over Lucky and hit him with three more in the chest. Lucky had to be dead before he even hit the pavement, but dude definitely made sure. The nigga that was in the passenger side jumped out of the car going off.

"Man, what the fuck is wrong with you! You trippin'!" Muncie jumped in the Lexus and smashed out of the parking lot doin' a buck 80, running over lucky's body, which was laid out in front of the car. This all happened in maybe 10 or 15 seconds. By the time it sunk in, what had just happened, Cookie was out the door wit a .45 in hand. He tried to hit the fleeing Lexus because he fired 4 rounds its way, but it was too far gone to get off a good shot. He ran over and cradled Lucky's body in his arms and cried for the Little Homie. As I came running out of the apartment, a red Ford Taurus and a mini-van pulled up and the same Narco's that had been jumping out on the neighborhood hustlers, jumped

RESPECT REVENGE Pt. 1
"When Naptown Couldn't Sleep"

out and surrounded Cookie. They had eight different hand canons aimed at his head in no time flat. They started yelling at him, "Drop the weapon and lay on your face! Do it now!" Cookie didn't even look up at em', he just sat there rockin' Lil Lucky's body for what seemed like an eternity. Then he laid Lucky down very gently and I thought he was going to surrender. He looked in my direction and I could read his mind. I knew he was choosing his own destiny. He quickly pointed his weapon at one of the officers and pulled the trigger 3 times, but I heard like fifty shots. They riddled my nigga's body with bullets. It was straight up overkill; family would definitely have to have a closed casket funeral. I slid back into the apartment without being seen. I cried out and flipped over every piece of furniture in that mufucka. I had just watched my two closest comrade's go to the grave in less than two minutes. Death was part of life, but my heart ached when I lost someone in my inner circle. I had lost everyone close to me in the last few years. First it was Big June, then Keisha, P.U. and now, both Lil Lucky and Cookie had died like dogs in the street. There was nothing that I could have done to prevent either death, but I didn't understand why Cookie decided to go out today. Then I remembered when he walked out of jail after beating them murders he said, he wasn't letting them people put him back in no cage, and I guess he meant that.

  I couldn't leave the apartment for like 12 hours because the police were out there processing the scene of the two dead gangsta's and the dead cop. They went door to door trying to see if anyone could shed some light on what had occurred prior to their arrival.

  They came up empty handed and when they came to the door of the apartment that I was in; I just simply didn't answer it.

RESPECT REVENGE Pt. 1
"When Naptown Couldn't Sleep"

I called the apartment where Juan-C and his partner was holed up at, and he said they were staying until they caught up with the nigga that we came to see. I waited until midnight and bounced in the S.T.S, leaving them with the truck.

RESPECT REVENGE Pt. 1
"When Naptown Couldn't Sleep"

CHAPTER 43

The ride back to the city was the longest couple hours of my life. I thought and reflected on every aspect of my life and the people in it. I thought about all of my dead folks and realized that every one of them that had died, didn't even realize that death was breathing down their neck until it was too late. Death gives you no warnings, it just gobbles you up. I had dealt in death for a while now, and seeing my men die that day struck something in me. When I made it to the crib, shit really started to unravel a lil bit. I should have saw the sign's, but I had been too caught up to pay any attention.

    I woke up next to Sheen the morning after I got back. She wasn't going in to the shop that day because she knew I wasn't right mentally after the loss of the guys. She laid there in the bed and held on to me while I tried to sort through the shit that was going on in my head. I knew I was going to hunt that nigga Muncie down if Juan-C didn't, for the way he had done Lil Lucky. But now wasn't the time, I was too fucked up. I stayed in the house for four whole days before I got up and hit the pavement.

    Cookie and Lucky's funerals were one day apart,

RESPECT REVENGE Pt. 1
"When Naptown Couldn't Sleep"

first Luck's then Cookie's. I was like a zombie during both. The whole hood was out to mourn the loss of two of the most feared and respected soldiers that the Hard-Part had ever bred. To see my dogs faces on people's shirts, it really hit home that they were gone. After Cookie's funeral and burial, which was in the same cemetery as Keisha's, I went over to lil cuz's grave and chilled with her for a while. Sheen just sat in the car watching me go through it.

      Everyone else had left, and I was alone until I looked up and saw a shadow standing over me. It was none other than E. Young, the homicide detective.
"So, have you lost or taken enough lives out here to give this shit up or what?"
I just looked at him through tear stained eyes. He kept at it.
"I told you, you always leave something behind everywhere you go. Now you done started leaving your trash in other states huh?"
As soon as he said it, I jumped up and was bout to take his head off his shoulders, but he put his hand on his pistol.
He said, "Go ahead, swing E! Give me a reason to make your family have to buy another plot out here!" I looked him in the eye and said,
"You ain't good enough for me to let you win! You better try and get somebody that don't know how to play this game if you want to solve cases. Cause fuckin' around and chasing me, you will be the laughing stock of the department!"
I was walking away, and he yelled to the back of my head,
"I'll have the last laugh; cause I know something that you don't know! You will get yours!"
The next day, I called Lil Dave and told him to meet me at the apartment building that I owned in the hood. He said that he would be there before I would. I hopped in Juan-C's S.T.S. and hit the hood.

RESPECT REVENGE Pt. 1
"When Naptown Couldn't Sleep"

When I pulled up, Lil Dave was standing around with the same nigga Rude and 3 other dudes that I didn't even know. I rolled down my window and said,
 "Jump in Lil Dave, let me holla at you!"
"Ain't nothin to holler about Lil Homie! Shit done changed round here since you been gone!"
I felt myself getting hot under the collar.
I said, "What you mean, we ain't got nothing to holler about? We got business!"
"We had business, but our business done came to an end!"
"So what you saying Lil Dave?"
"I think you know what I'm saying nigga! You might as well bounce! There is a new Sherriff in town!"
Then he turned his back as if to say he was through talkin' bout it. The four nigga's he was with stood up and lifted their shirts, exposing the butts of their guns. I laughed at these pretenders, and pulled off.
I couldn't win right then, but I was a seasoned veteran at this drama shit, and I ain' t never been took for nothing and I wasn't gettin' ready to start now.

    The game is a dog eat dog situation. When a predator smells blood, they move in for the kill. Even a predator could become prey when he was weak or wounded. By me losing my whole squad, he figured me to be weak. He had 15 bricks to feed his hyena's and he felt like he had the upper hand. I called Harvey, B-Boy, and Lil Kev and they told me that the nigga been preaching this take over shit since the day everybody found out that Cookie and Lucky was dead. I was being forced out; at least that is what they thought.

RESPECT REVENGE Pt. 1
"When Naptown Couldn't Sleep"

CHAPTER 44

I owned 14 houses in my hood. I had been buying abandoned or condemned houses and fixing them up for a while by that point. Some were occupied, some were not. I had at least one unoccupied on every block where we sold dope in the hood. So for the next 30 days, I would wait until the late night and ease into the back door of one of the houses and stash at least one chopper and one pistol. The nigga's only sold dope on five different blocks, plus on Burton Ave. I'm the one who set the hood up like it was, they must have forgot. I had all the bases covered besides Burton Ave., but Ms. Jones lived on Burton Ave. and she loved her some Lil E. Even more than that, she loved money. I bought her a cell phone and got a key made to her back door. I paid her $1,000 to be my eyes and ears of her block. Once everything was in place, I was ready to bang. I was getting ready to wage war on my own hood, from the inside out.

  The first night of action was relatively simple. I crept in my spot on 26th St., grabbed a chopper and made hell a reality for all those hanging out on the block. I had on all black. Black jeans, black hoodie sweatshirt, and some black

RESPECT REVENGE Pt. 1
"When Naptown Couldn't Sleep"

Air Max's. I had taken it back to the basics. It was 10 or 12 nigga's hangin' out on the block wit white T's on, sellin' dope without a care in the world. When I came off the side of that house, it was like they had seen a ghost. I came out lettin' em' have it. **Chop-Chop-Chop**, it sounded like a thunder storm out that bitch. In between shots, I was yelling out,

"26th Street is closed for business! Ain't no hanging out round here!"

Then I would go back to chopping. **Chop-Chop-Chop**. Nigga's was fallin or flyin'. They was trying to get somewhere with the quickness. I didn't even see their faces, just T-shirts. When I got finished, 6 lay sprawled out, and I took off down the alley and into the back door of my next crib.

I didn't have nothing in these houses but fresh carpet and guns. I would let a day or two pass before I put down my next episode, but every time they tried to hang on the next block, I would come and tear it up. Somebody had told on me because the homicide dick had been at my lawyer, Sheen, Granny and Ty. But my peoples wasn't offering no assistance to the law.

I guess the nigga's in the hood felt like this shit had gone on long enough because I got a call on my phone from a lil nigga named L-Roy, he told me that the nigga Lil Dave could be found in the trunk of a car parked on the dead end. L-Roy said that he had held him down and made him talk, and in the process, he had come up on 6 bricks. What did I want him to do with it?

"Listen my nigga. You earned that, good lookin on handling that lil business, so take that as a payment for your work, and for keepin' it real. You be careful, and run the hood with an iron fist, or one of them nigga's will try you."

For that whole month, I had been like a ghost in the hood, but it wasn't Casper because it wasn't nothing friendly about it. My mind had went blank. I'd taken all the pain that I had bottle

RESPECT REVENGE Pt. 1
"When Naptown Couldn't Sleep"

up inside of me, out on anyone and everyone that I thought was associated with Lil Dave. If you weren't with me, you were against me, and I was alone in this battle field. I had caused all hustling to come to an abrupt halt. Nigga's started trying to play the streets a little bit in the day time, but the nights belonged to me. From sun down until sun up, I had prowled the hood taking aim at anything brave enough to test the waters. Most were terrified, but respected my position with this shit. I had sacrificed a lot to bring money to the hood. I put money on the books of anyone who got locked up. I didn't allow nobody to bring drama into our borders, unless it was us. I brought the hood up as I came up, only to be betrayed by the same nigga's that I showed love to. I was glad when I had gotten the call from L-Roy saying that he had got the nigga Lil Dave, and came up on 6 bricks in the process because I was tired. Even after that, I would walk the streets of my ghetto on the late nighters, and I would see the detectives or regular beat cops riding down the empty streets with their spot lights shined between the houses, and I knew they were looking for me, but I would just duck off in the shadows and blow a spiff of that purple, and think about all that I had been through ...

RESPECT REVENGE Pt. 1
"When Naptown Couldn't Sleep"

CHAPTER
45

A few nights later, the detectives reached out to the local media for help getting me off of the streets. They had a local news anchor do a story on me, hoping to put enough pressure on whoever they thought was harboring me, to turn me in. I sat in the house of my last known ally in the hood, Ms. Jones, and watched the news myself. It came on at exactly 11:00 p.m. The news theme music came on, then it said, Live, local, late breaking. Good evening Indianapolis. The Indianapolis Police Department's homicide unit needs your help in getting one of the worst criminals that the city has ever seen, off the streets tonight. I have here with me, Homicide Detective Eric Young from the west district. Good evening detective, could you tell us exactly what we are dealing with here?"

"I'll tell you what you are dealing with, he is death itself. Who we are talking about is 25-year-old Eric Hunt, but the streets know him as "Big E." He is from a local street gang known as the HardPart. He is without question, the leader of the murderous, violent street organization. He has been involved in murder, robbery, kidnaping, extortion, and high level drug dealing for many years now. We had not been

RESPECT REVENGE Pt. 1
"When Naptown Couldn't Sleep"

able to get to him for years because he kept himself insulated by surrounding himself with loyal individuals that flourished financially while under his leadership. He is directly responsible for or connected to as many as twenty to twenty-five murders in this city in the last eight years. We have reason to believe that he has dealt in death, in as many as four other Midwestern cities. We had two witnesses identify his top two lieutenants some time back, putting them in jail for murder, only to have who we believe was Mr. Hunt himself kill the informant, who also happened to be his best friend. So he doesn't play by rules, besides the ones he makes himself. Up until now, he hadn't given us anything to use that would be helpful in aiding in his prosecution. Then he enacted a war against the very same gang that he used to run, single handedly killing at least 9 individuals, and critically wounding at least a half a dozen more. But he finally left a witness alive who is willing to help us bring him to justice. We have this person in a safe house for fear of retaliation for his cooperation with the authorities. Now all we need is the public's help in capturing him, before he kills again. Here is a recent photo of Mr. Hunt, taken just months ago at the funeral of his top lieutenant Jevin Cummings, a.k.a. Lil Lucky. The Mayor and the city of Indianapolis has labeled this man an "Urban Terrorist" and have started a massive manhunt for him. The fugitive taskforce, which is a state, local, and federal unified entity, will capture him eventually. If anyone has any information on the whereabouts of this man, I urge you to dial 272-tips. You can remain anonymous and be eligible for a cash reward of up to $10,000 dollars. Again that number is 272-tips. Thank you."

    "Thank you detective. This has been Steven Shepherd reporting live for channel 6 news. Now back to you in the studio Jim. "

Ms. Jones was sitting there with tears rolling down her face.

RESPECT REVENGE Pt. 1
"When Naptown Couldn't Sleep"

She said, "They painted an ugly picture of you Lil E. They even called you an "Urban Terrorist". Someone is going to try and collect that money off of you, watch what I tell you."
I got up and gave Ms. Jones a hug and told her thanks for everything. I gave her a rubber band with $1,500 in it, and told her to take care of herself, I knew that this would be my last visit. I slid out of the backdoor and disappeared into the night. I called Tyesha and told her to go get Granny, my son, and Sheen, and meet me at the safe house that I had set up on the Northside.

RESPECT REVENGE Pt. 1
"When Naptown Couldn't Sleep"

CHAPTER 46

When I walked into the house, everyone was already there. My son was laying on the couch sleep, looking just like me. Ty and Sheen never had much to say to each other prior to today, but they had put all of that to the side for the sake of the situation. I hugged all three of the ladies in my life, and told them that no matter what the future held, they would all be financially secure no matter what. I had amassed three successful businesses, each helping a member of my family solidify their financial standings. Plus, I owned 14 houses, and two 16-unit apartment buildings in the neighborhood. Then I had cash in safe deposit boxes in each of their names.

 I gave them each their individual time, starting with Sheen and my son. She woke him up and we went off into a bedroom in the back. She sat on the bed and her tears started flowing freely. She said,

 "Baby, you know I love you, and I 've always loved you. Whatever you decide to do, or need me to do, I 'm with you 100%, even if I have to deal with Tyesha. I know that you love me, and I know you love her too, so I accept that. Your son worships the ground that you walk on. I feel the sorriest

RESPECT REVENGE Pt. 1
"When Naptown Couldn't Sleep"

for him in this situation. Whatever you need, we are here."
She got up and hugged me, and we stood in the middle of the floor and cried together. Me, her and Baby Eric. I said,
"I have a way to get out of town and be set up where I could not be found. Once I'm settled in, I'm a send for you okay? "
"Okay."
She touched my face, kissed my lips, and told me to be careful. Next, I called my granny in the room. It broke my heart to see her looking the way she was looking. She was trying to be strong, but that didn't last long. She cried while she talked to me.

"Well baby, you are at a crossroad right now. Every decision or move that you make is detrimental to the outcome of your life. This is the life that you chose to lead, and in the very beginning I told you that it plays for keeps. There ain't nothing that I can do for you now, besides pray. God is the only one who can fix this mess. He is the deliverer. You got to pray and ask him to forgive you for all you have done, and ask for his guidance. You have separated yourself from his mercy, and you have allowed the devil to take control, but God will forgive you. Pray with me."
For the first time since I was 8 years old, I was on my knees with my granny, praying. I hoped she was right, because I felt like I didn't have many options left, so giving a prayer for thanks, and asking for help from God, couldn't hurt me anymore than I was hurting now. After the prayer, she got up and hugged me, then grabbed both sides of my face and said,

"You be safe out there you hear me? Don't let nobody take your life from you. I'd rather visit you in the jail, than in a grave. Always respect revenge baby. Don't ever think you are so bad or untouchable where no one can get you okay. I know we wasn't the only ones to see that news. Everybody got someone who loves them, and that news show may have brought back old feelings for some people. Just be careful."

RESPECT REVENGE Pt. 1
"When Naptown Couldn't Sleep"

I hugged her tight to my body and said,
    "I will Granny, and I love you."
Tyesha came into the room after Granny had left, she looked like she had lost her best friend. She looked at me and said,
    "Hi baby."
I grabbed her arm and pulled her close.
"How you holding up baby girl?" I could feel her body shaking, she said,
"I'm not holding up; I feel like I'm emotionally dead right now."
"Did you bring what I asked you to bring?"
"Yeah, it's in there in the front room."
I told her to bring my get away bags. I had kept two bags with clothes and a gun, plus some fake I.D. I also had some other essentials in there too. In the other bag was enough cash to hold me
in any situation that may arise. I knew that one day, it might come to this, so I had a plan in affect. Earlier, I had contacted Raul down in Miami, and told him that I needed him to put me away for a while. He told me that he could hide a person forever if need be. He had a system in place, a bunch of remote compounds and safe houses for these type of situations. He said all I needed to do was get to him and I would be straight, then I could send for those closest to me. All of those were in this apartment with me now. Ty was catching a late flight to Atlanta, where my Auntie Rhonda had transportation waiting for her. Then she would drive the rest of the way to Miami. I sent Sheen, my son, and my Granny on home and told them that I would be in touch as soon as I got situated. We said our goodbyes, and they left the apartment.

RESPECT REVENGE Pt. 1
"When Naptown Couldn't Sleep"

CHAPTER
47

I picked up the phone and called the phone that was only to be used between me and Jake, Juan- C answered.
"Yeah, what 's up?"
I said, "Where Jake at?"
"He out of town right now, he left me with all of the phones."
"Look, I got a problem and I'm a need you to help a nigga out. I need to get to Lexington, Kentucky tonight, but I can't get there the regular way. I need you to come through with the F-150 and tuck me off in the spot, you feel me?"
"Yeah, that ain't no problem. I saw the lil situation on T.V., so I already know what's up."
"So you got me?"
He said, "Yeah, how long before you be ready to ride?"
"Just give me an hour. I'll be ready to go"
I gave him the directions to the spot, and he said that he would pick me up in an hour.
   The F-150 would come in handy for real this time, instead of coke in the stash spot, it would be me. He would get me safely out of Indiana, where every police agency was riding around with my picture on the dash of their cars. He

RESPECT REVENGE Pt. 1
"When Naptown Couldn't Sleep"

would drive me to Lexington, Kentucky where I would switch vehicles, and get into one that Raul's people down there had waiting for me in a designated spot. I would make the drive to Florida from there with the help of my fake I.D. Once in Florida, I would be in the hands of my man Raul.

While we waited for the hour to pass, me and Ty talked about life and what we could make of the one's that we were living. She said that she didn't give a damn if we had to live in a cave, as long as she was with me.

I said, "It won't come to that, but it might not be the fairy-tale ending that you dreamed of as a little girl."

"I knew that when I chose to be your girl, with yo crazy ass."

She managed through tears. She was a good girl and she deserved a better life, and I knew this situation wasn't fair to her, but we don't choose who we love. That is left up to the heart, and our hearts had made a connection, that not even this situation could break. I knew once we made it to Miami and got settled in, I would not want to let her stray far from my side. When your heart becomes as hard as mines had become, you need something to balance your hate. The only thing that can fight hate is love, and she was my equalizer.

When she started to realize that my ride would be there any minute, she started to get nervous again.

She said, "Baby, I don't want to leave your side. Why don't you just let me drive us to Florida?"

"Because, if the police pull us over anywhere in this state, your name alone will make them check and see who I am with more scrutiny, and my fake I.D. will be useless. I know they have put a red flag on your name because they know you are close to me. They expect us to make a break for the airport or the highway, which we are, but not the way that they expect."

RESPECT REVENGE Pt. 1
"When Naptown Couldn't Sleep"

She said, "I trust you, but I have a feeling in the pit of my stomach that something ain't right."
"I got the same feeling baby girl. It's called anxiety. It's normal in situations like this.
Here, hit some of this Michael Jordan, and relax your nerves."
"Why do you call this weed Michael Jordan?"
"Because, it will take you up high, and keep you floatin' for a while."
She laughed at my lil joke, and it lightened the mood a lil bit.
I said, "Trust me baby, everything a be a'ight, and this shit will soon be behind us. It will never disappear, but we will be able to deal with it better from afar."

My phone rang, it was Juan-C.

"I'm outside, come on down."

I said, "A'ight, give me a second."
I hugged baby girl tight to my body and kissed her on the top of her head.
"I'll see you in a couple of days okay?" She started right back up.
"Why can't I go with you now?"
"We already been through this Tyesha. You got to trust me."
She started to say, "I do trust you but...."
"But nothing, just stick to the plan."
I grabbed my bags and headed towards the door. Baby held it open for me and I walked down the steps to begin my three-day journey to a new life.

RESPECT REVENGE Pt. 1
"When Naptown Couldn't Sleep"

CHAPTER 48

I put my bags in the back of the truck, then opened the door and got in. As soon as I closed the door, I saw this bright flash of light, like how lightning lights up the night sky. At the same time, I heard a boom that sounded damn near like thunder. I figured that the laws had caught up wit a nigga, and maybe it was a flash grenade or something. Then, there was no sound at all, just images from my life flashing through my mind. It was all playing out in slow motion, but in reality, all this took place in a fraction of a second. Then, it was like I wasn't in my body anymore. I was looking at all this from a detached view point. I could see Juan-C looking over at me with a grimace on his face. I could see his man in the backseat, who hadn't even had time to pull his hand back yet. I could even see the .357 snub nose that was still smoking in his hand. Then, I saw myself. Still in my seat, but slumped over the dash, a hole in the back of my head, my forehead was wide open. I had blood running down my face and brains were all over the windshield. My eyes were wide open, but staring at nothing.

So, this is death huh? I never felt it, and damn sure

RESPECT REVENGE Pt. 1
"When Naptown Couldn't Sleep"

wasn't expecting it. The first thought after seeing myself laying there dead was, why? Why would Juan-C have me killed? Then, as if a higher power was answering my question, a series of events flashed through my mind's eye like a movie.

    I was 16 again, riding with Money and had just gotten a page from Sheen. I asked Money could I use his phone, and he spoke into it and said,
"Juan-C, let me hit you back later, my lil nigga gotta use this phone. Man, you better swing past and see pops, he been asking about you."

    As soon as that scene was over, the next one popped up. Me beating pops Coleman in the face with my .45. Then it flipped again. Me and Jake talking in the V.I.P. section of the Mecca when he first introduced me to Juan-C.

    "Big E, this is Juan-C, Juan, Big E."
Then he got up and excused himself from the table. I felt a bad vibe off of him, but had overlooked it. The next scene was strange to me until I heard the words coming out of her mouth. It was Granny.

    "When you in them streets on any level, you are subject to anything that come with it. But when you work every day and are not involved in that foolishness, then it should never reach you doorstep. I don't know if you did it, or even just allowed it, but who ever had a hand in the beating death of that older fella over on Tacoma, was dead wrong."

Then me and Juan-C was on the highway, on our way to Louisville, and got pulled over by the state trooper. The trooper had said it for me as plain as day.

"Dejuan Coleman is it? Where are you in such a rush to get to?"
The final scene was Granny again, just an hour earlier.

 "Don't let nobody take your life from you. I'd rather visit you in the jail, than in the grave. Always **Respect Revenge baby.**"

RESPECT REVENGE Pt. 1
"When Naptown Couldn't Sleep"

And that's exactly what I hadn't done. All the signs were there, but I was too busy worried about something else every time one presented itself for me to see.

It turned out that Dejuan Coleman, a.k.a. "Juan-C", was Money's cousin from the eastside. That made him the nephew of Pops Coleman. I didn't die for killing Money, that is part of the game. I was killed for taking death to the doorstep of the innocent. I died for not respecting the game. I died for not **Respecting Revenge ...**

RESPECT REVENGE Pt. 1
"When Naptown Couldn't Sleep"

EPILOGUE

The Funeral . . .

The funeral home was packed to capacity. They had to open up another room to accommodate all of the people that had shown up at the last viewing of one of the Westside's finest. The HardPart was in there deep, as well as a lot of people who had shown up just to see the so called "Urban Terrorist" in the flesh.

    On the front row, Ms. Caroline (Lil E's grandmother), Tyesha, Sheen, and Baby Eric, sat in disbelief as they watched the procession of on lookers file past the casket, getting their last look at the young O.G. Tyesha and Sheen sat arm in arm behind dark Gucci shades, rocking back and forth, offering each other the support that they knew they would need in order to get through this situation.

    As the end of the line was in sight, and the preacher prepared to deliver his eulogy, Sheen suddenly felt Tyesha go stiff and squeeze her arm almost to the point of pain. Sheen leaned over and said into Ty's ear,

    "Girl, are you okay? What's wrong?"

Ty acted as if she didn't even hear her, and reached up and pulled off her shades. Her glare was focused on the tall dark

RESPECT REVENGE Pt. 1
"When Naptown Couldn't Sleep"

skinned dude with the dreads, standing beside Lil E's casket with Jake. Sheen followed her gaze, and looked at the two men standing at the casket. She didn't know either one of them, but something about them had Ty's undivided attention. Tyesha's expression had went from the hurt and pain one feels after the loss of a loved one, to pure anger and hate. As the men left the casket and headed their way, Ty slid her glasses back down on her face. Jake and Juan-C walked straight to Ty and Jake bent down and said into Ty's ear,

"You know 'Big E was my man. If there is anything I can do let me know."
As he talked, and Juan-C stood off to the side, tears rolled down her face like rain drops on a window pane. Tyesha got up and stormed out, and Sheen was fast on her heels to make sure that she was okay. When Sheen finally caught up to her in the bathroom, Ty had broken down and was crying hysterically.

"What's wrong Ty? What is it?"
"That's him girl! The dark skinned one with the dreads! He the one that came to pick Eric up that night! He killed him!"

Sheen could not believe her ears. That bastard had the nerves to show up here. He must have thought that no one knew. Eric had taught her better than to reveal her hand before it was time, so she helped Ty get herself together and said,
"Don't worry about it girl. He gonna get his. Don't say nothing to nobody okay?"
Ty shook her head up and down, and they stepped out of the bathroom and headed back to the service.

When they stepped into the hallway, L-Roy was standing there leaning against the wall. He walked up to Sheen and gave her a hug.
"How you doin' Sheen?"
"I'm tore up about it. I really can't believe he is gone."

RESPECT REVENGE Pt. 1
"When Naptown Couldn't Sleep"

  L-Roy said, "Yeah, me either. But check it, my man always been good to me, and he blessed me real strong before he died, I owe him a lot. If you or your son need anything, I'm here. Here go my number. Use it Sheen, even if it's just to let me be there a lil bit for Baby Eric. Lil- E was the realest and I'm not going to let the hood forget it. I'm gonna rep' my man to the fullest. If there is anything I can do, just say the word and it's done!"

  Sheen was from the hood too, so she knew that L-Roy wasn't faking when he expressed how he felt about Lil-E. A lot of them dudes over there didn't like Eric, but all of them respected him. Sheen hugged L-Roy and turned to leave, but as she did, she couldn't help but wonder if when L-Roy said just say the word and it'll be done, did that include murder? However it went, she would see to it that Juan-C didn't get away with the murder of her baby's father, she owed him that much. She tucked L-Roy's number into her pocket, grabbed Ty's hand, and went back to take their seats ...

RESPECT REVENGE Pt. 1
"When Naptown Couldn't Sleep"

SHOCK-G

RESPECT REVENGE Pt. 1
"When Naptown Couldn't Sleep"

LETTER FROM
THE AUTHOR

" I wrote this particular series of books. (Respect Revenge Series) not as a glorification of anything street, but as a testament to the realities of the underworld. There are many levels to the "game" and all of them end in misery in one way at the other. Look at lil E? He was winning and was a thinker and had it going for himself. (Or so it seemed) How did that turn out for him? What about his baby momma Sheen? She's left to raise a man-child on her own in this cruel world and his son is now a fatherless one. How about his girl Ty? She gave her heart to a man and they were building a life together; now she to is left to pick up the pieces of her life alone. How about his team? Cookie, P.U. and Lil Lucky? All DEAD!!! How bout lil Smurf and money? What about Big June? Are you catching on yet? This book is full of lessons and the main one being that you get what you give or you reap what you sew out here and there is no affect that can come forth without cause. If you in the streets sewing bad seeds all day everyday, what should you reasonably expect to come forth from them?

RESPECT REVENGE Pt. 1
"When Naptown Couldn't Sleep"

What about Keisha? She wasn't sewing bad seeds, but still met her end as if she had. Brutally murdered like she was a gangsta in the streets herself. Do you not realize that other people's Karma will come back to them and if you happen to be in the way when it shows up at their doorsteps, Karma will not discriminate at all. What about their grandmother? Yeah she is still alive, but she a victim none the less because she had to bury 2 grandchildren in a very short period of time. Did she ask for or deserve that? This series is called Respect Revenge but it could have simply been titled "THAT'S LAW" because everything in the book deals with law. Rules change but Law does not...

-Shock-G

RESPECT REVENGE Pt. 1
"When Naptown Couldn't Sleep"

ABOUT THE AUTHOR

Shane "Zulu" Shepherd is a self-made business man who wears many hats, including, but not limited to Boss, Author, Inspirational Speaker and Leader of the team. He writes both fiction and nonfiction literature at which times he uses different pseudonyms, depending on which form of his art he is currently engaged.

When writing fictional literature (as in his RESPECT REVENGE series) he goes by the name Shock-G. When he lifts his thoughts to higher levels of consciousness and writes his non-fiction works (such as TRUTH and CHANGE) he writes under the name G. Zulu. Mr. Shepherd is determined to win and lives by the motto: PROPER PREPARATION PREVENTS A POOR PERFORMANCE and that's LAW!!!

RESPECT REVENGE Pt. 1
"When Naptown Couldn't Sleep"

COMING SOON
FROM H.A.R.D P.A.R.T PUBLISHING

"Respect Revenge Pt.2" (Fiction)

RESPECT REVENGE Pt. 1
"When Naptown Couldn't Sleep"

COMING SOON
FROM H.A.R.D P.A.R.T PUBLISHING

"Respect Revenge Pt.3" (Fiction)

RESPECT REVENGE Pt. 1
"When Naptown Couldn't Sleep"

COMING SOON
FROM H.A.R.D P.A.R.T PUBLISHING

"The Game you can't win and the untold truth about it" (Non-Fiction)

COMING SOON
FROM H.A.R.D P.A.R.T PUBLISHING

"Truth and Change... Knowledge, Wisdom and Understanding for and about the young Black Male" (Non-Fiction)

COMING SOON
FROM H.A.R.D P.A.R.T PUBLISHING

"The immeasurable value and effortless beauty of the Black Woman" (Non-Fiction)

RESPECT REVENGE Pt. 1
"When Naptown Couldn't Sleep"

RESPECT REVENGE Pt. 1
"When Naptown Couldn't Sleep"

RESPECT REVENGE Pt. 1
"When Naptown Couldn't Sleep"

RESPECT REVENGE Pt. 1
"When Naptown Couldn't Sleep"

RESPECT REVENGE Pt. 1
"When Naptown Couldn't Sleep"